ADVANCE PRAISE FOR
GIVE UNTO US

"Justin Lutz, this generation's Michael McDowell, proves yet again that he is here to bash our minds with stories so wonderfully—almost gleefully—grotesque, and made all the more grotesque by the empathy with which he explores his characters and their worlds. *Give Unto Us* is immediate, wry, and made me literally squirm, as if gritty sand were being elbowed into a hot, septic wound in my side. Oh, and it's tenderly romantic at times. This is a story of love and parental anxiety and pus, written by such an empathetic writer whose work is so alive, and so very frightening. I loved it."

—Aaron Dries,
author of *Dirty Heads* and *House of Sighs*

"*Give Unto Us* is Justin Lutz deftly edging his fingers under the edge of a scab while distracting you with gorgeous prose—a sage song of syllable and word—until the precise moment comes when he rips it free and lets us bleed freely. His novella of family and worry, of holes, both literal and metaphorical-binding the wound. It's essential reading teaming with emotions, horrors and sand. It's brilliant."

—John Boden,
author of *Snarl* and *Jedi Summer*

GIVE UNTO US

JUSTIN LUTZ

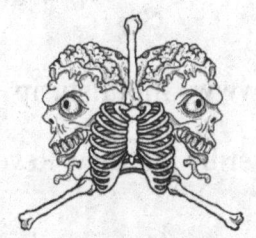

Ghoulish Books
San Antonio, Texas

Give Unto Us
Copyright © 2024 Justin Lutz

First Edition

All Rights Reserved

ISBN: 978-1-943720-99-6

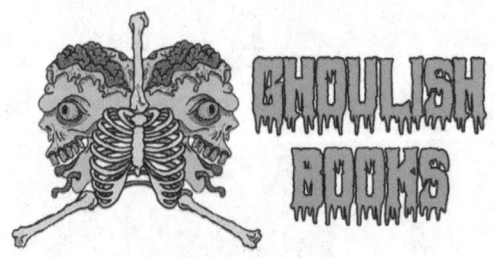

www.Ghoulish.rip

Cover by Matthew Revert

ALSO BY THE AUTHOR

Gemini Rising
Hold My Hand and Hope For Heaven
ACAB Includes Animal Control
Void Haus (with the Void Collective)
Gone To Seed

for Lois, the queen of our (sand) castle

There's a hole in my bucket, dear Liza, dear Liza,
There's a hole in my bucket, dear Liza, a hole.

—camp song

1.

IT'S THE RIVER that finally sells him: a meandering snake weaving through the sunken back quadrant of the yard, separated by a steep forty-foot drop.

"We'd have to put a fence up," Melissa says, and Trevor nods, but he's already in a kayak with a beer in hand, already pouring a concrete pad and building a gazebo, already priming the grill and carrying out hamburgers and packets of cheese.

"It's actually a win-win," Tammy says. Tammy is a squat bull-dog of a realtor, an over-positive whirlwind that has dragged them from house to house blatantly ignoring their wish-list. "You butt up right against the river, but because of the incline, you won't need flood insurance."

Trevor could give a shit about flood insurance, could give a shit about fences, what he gives a shit about is that despite the flaws, despite the slopped-on white paint thick as linoleum and despite the cracked sidewalk and despite the crumbling stone basement, he wants this house. He wants to mow this lawn, hang clothing on this wash line, and he wants to build a set of stairs down this steep incline to the river. He's never had a boat and never swung a hammer, but he is already envisioning the floating dock he will build.

"We'll have to keep an eye on Brody—he could easily fall down this bank, slide into the river, turn up in Philadelphia," Melissa says.

Trevor knows that the joke at the end of that statement

is her way of deflecting the worry she feels, and he knows that a fence for the top of the drop to the river will be the first item on his honey-do list.

"How wild does that place get?" Trevor asks, gesturing with his chin at a restaurant separated from their house only by a large yard. A weathered sign out front christens it the All-Weather Bar and Grill.

"It's a family place, from what I understand," Tammy says, but Trevor can see a nervous twitch crawling to the space behind her eyes, burrowing in like a parasite. He turns to Melissa.

"We'll probably want to put in a fence. Your dad can help with that, yeah?"

She nods, and Tammy looks reassured, says, "Why don't the two of you take a moment and talk it over. I'll be in the kitchen when you're ready." She smiles that realtor smile she's so good at, the bullshit seeping brown between her teeth. When she retreats to the house, Trevor turns to his wife.

"I think I want this one, Miss," he says, and she smiles.

"I was hoping you'd say that. There's plenty wrong with it, but it's not so far gone that it can't be a project house, even for us."

Unspoken between them, but felt by both, is that the property seems to radiate, pulse, hum, as if something in the universe is calling them here, holding up a neon sign.

"Exactly what I was thinking." He looks at his watch. "How long do you want to let Tammy sweat?"

"Honestly, after some of the hell-holes she made us tour, I'm tempted to go for fries and a beer at the bar."

He puts his arm around her, and they stand in the yard—*their* yard—looking down at the slow run of the river like time slipping through the fingers of the world.

They move in during the warm embrace of Indian summer, tendrils of late afternoon sun penetrating the windows and casting shadows in the corners of the large living room, dust swirling in the glow.

2.

THE PLACE THEY leave is an apartment nestled in the creeping bloat of the city, a starter home whose walls began closing in on them the moment they brought Brody home from the hospital.

The new house, which Trevor already refers to as the River House and the Waterfront Property, is palatial in comparison—big downstairs rooms spilling into each other with wanton grace and a cozy, carpeted second floor that feels like home the second they place their bed in the master. It sits on a half-acre of land, a plot that Trevor describes to friends and family as not his preferred "retire-and-die-on-it" sized parcel, but it's a start. Halfway back are two large, drooping pine trees that obscure the back end of the yard. Hollenbach Road in front of the house runs parallel to the river. The Grubers occupy a modest two story on the East side of the property. The All-Weather Bar and Grill sits on the West.

Trevor digs into home improvement projects with a rare zeal, knowing that the sooner the house is up to standards, the sooner Melissa will look the other way in regard to his reckless river passion projects. He buys paint, and the three of them touch up the scuffs and scrapes accrued by the movers, two-year-old Brody's support more moral than practical. On one of his trips to the hardware store, he buys flexible aluminum fencing and a grip of stakes to line the lip of the bank out back, knowing full well that they will sit in the shed until he further examines the river access option.

3

The property management company that Tammy works for made sure the property was landscaped in a way that would entice new buyers—fresh mulch, mowed lawn, clipped shrubs—so it's almost two full weeks before Trevor pulls his rust-speckled hand-me-down push mower from the shed at the back of the property and fires it up.

At first he takes his time, tries to soak it in, tries to find contentment in the simple tasks that accompany home ownership, but soon he's annoyed by things he failed to notice on their myriad tours of the house. Parts of the yard are uneven, divots and ruts accented by holes burrowed by free-loading chipmunks. He sees a fast-food napkin too late, and it's sucked into the blades of the mower only to reappear as trashy confetti, greasy shreds that sprinkle the grass. He pauses to look up to the restaurant, its lot dotted with the cars of afternoon diners and day-drinkers, and resolves to meet the owner and say something about the lids of their dumpsters.

The fence can't go up soon enough.

A maple tree in the front yard that he found so charming before is now a challenging tangle of above-ground roots that he stumbles through. Chips of wood fly from the mower when the blades connect, and he swears and stops the motor. Melissa is standing on the side porch when he rounds the house, her eyes asking what's wrong and her hand holding a beer. He cracks it and takes a swig, choosing to delay answering her unspoken question.

"There are a bunch of projects out here, too," he says, wiping foam from his mustache of stubble. "I think we should call around and get that fence up sooner than later. I didn't realize the trash from the restaurant would blow over here. I already hit a napkin and blew it to pieces."

Rather than share in his misery, Melissa laughs, the sound buoying him out of the dark sea he's allowed his mind to sink into. "If that's the least of our problems, I think we're doing pretty good." She throws her arms around his neck and kisses him hard. "We bought a goddamn house, Trev. You and me. Together. We knew it wouldn't be easy, but would you rather be back in the apartment?"

"With John downstairs starting his construction projects at six am?"

"And that endless pack of pitbulls barking next door," she says.

"Don't forget the giant pothole in front of the building that every semi-truck made sure to hit." He smiles, aware of what she's doing but welcoming it all the same. The balance is part of what he loves about her, her uncanny ability to lift him out of his intrusive thought pattern and bring him back to a grateful place. It never fails, and he is always surprised that he can be so negative and grateful that she sees something hiding in his tough outer shell and surly bouts of pouting self-doubt.

Five years of marriage has fostered this dynamic, his anxiety, lingering depression, and penchant for overthinking a tight-rope act above her reassuring net.

She takes the empty can from him and squeezes, the aluminum crunching in her hand. "Brody is full-on into a nap, so if you hurry and finish the yard, maybe we can hop into the shower before he wakes up." She grabs the billow of his shirt and pulls until his lips meet hers.

"Yes, ma'am!" He mock-salutes and restarts the mower, the beer giving him a second wind. She winks and melts back into the house, the screen door clacking behind her.

Any pretense of basking in labor is gone now, and he rushes through the backyard, clipping the grass in shaky uneven rows. Thoughts of Melissa splayed on the bed upstairs already half-dressed fill his mind, and his steps quicken thinking of the rare window of time without Brody's needs filling their immediate future, a window of time that echoes what their life was like before.

Trevor didn't want to be a father, not really, but he always held the belief that if and when it happened his heart would flip a switch in his brain that would endear him to it. They agreed, early on in their relationship, that they didn't want kids, that they wanted to live the freewheeling life abandoned by their peers and carry on traveling, saving money, and living as they saw fit. As the years passed, he assumed it a foregone conclusion, something they didn't need mention, and when the tiny plus sign appeared on the pregnancy test, it was the cross atop the grave of his ambitions. Here lie all the mountains never climbed, the books never written, the exotic meals never eaten.

The things he'll never do coagulated within him, form a black mass, an unfillable hole, a chunk of missing soul that he blamed on Brody.

For the first few weeks after Brody is born, Trevor was able to push these feelings aside and be present for his son. He pulled his share of middle-of-the-night duty, walking the child in circles around the apartment while midnight traffic thundered and bumped through the potholes in front of the building. He found a new job copywriting for a company in Atlanta that allowed him to go full-remote other than a few video conferences a month, and he doesn't even mind when Brody interrupts those with his incessant, needy wails.

At some point in Brody's second year, he noticed that the switch had flipped back.

At first he thought it was the apartment—that the confined space had caused him to grow cold, had turned his son into a breathing, farting nuisance—so when they find the house and settle on it, his mood improves, he drinks fewer beers at the end of the day, he starts to jog.

The house, he thinks, will be a fresh start, a new way to enjoy life, and another chance to learn to love his son.

He pushes hard in the home stretch, the shed a few feet away and the lip of the river in view.

Just before he pulls even with the shed, his right foot sinks a few inches into the yard. He has time to think *fuck, that's a big chipmunk hole* before he trips and sinks to his knees. Ownership of his right ankle stays with the hole, and he feels a sharp pain as it twists, strains, crunches. A shout escapes his mouth, and he shoves the handle of the mower and uses his hands to catch himself in the soft lawn. The mower, free of his hands, continues for half a foot before shutting off and coming to a stop.

The clack of the screen door sounds again as if to bookend his embarrassment, and he hears Melissa call out, her bare feet pounding the yard behind him. He tries to stand, and his ankle fills with fire, the pain sending him back down to earth.

She reaches him and takes hold of his calf.

"Okay, Trev, hold still, one, two, three."

His ankle pops free, and he flips to his back, panting. She pulls off his shoe and uses it to prop his leg up, the ankle already starting to discolor and swell.

"Are you okay? Do you think it's broken?"

He winces and tries to rotate his ankle.

"I've still got movement, but I think it's sprained. Hurts like a motherfucker. What the hell did I step in?"

Trevor tries to sit up, and Melissa puts a gentle hand on his chest.

"Just lie down. I'll look."

She pivots to the hole, brushes grass clippings from the opening.

"It looks like it's sand, actually." Unconsciously, she looks to the lip of the yard, the drop, the river. "Do you think the ground here has sand leaching up from the riverbank? This far up?"

He doesn't know what he thinks, not yet, just knows that his ankle hurts, fucking *screams,* and that his head has begun pulsing in grisly rhythm with the pulse of blood in his leg.

She digs in the sand, pulling handfuls out and setting them next to the opening, and for the first few scoops all he can think is that the sand isn't the pressing issue here.

Didn't she see him, hear him, feel him crush his ankle? Can't she see him lying here in the grass, emasculated and immobilized?

"Hon, that might be the sand mound for the septic tank. I wouldn't get too wild digging in there."

"Nah, I thought that too, but we're on sewer."

Her hand is submerged up the wrist, and her tongue sticks out of the side of her mouth in concentration until her eyes widen, and she pulls something blue and plastic from the hole. Trevor's rage dissipates as quickly as it appeared, the curiosity of the object and the glee in her smile pushing it out of his pulsing head.

She brushes sand from the artifact and holds it out to him. A plastic shovel, weathered and scratched with age.

"There's our answer. The old owners must have had kids. Maybe they dumped a sandbox or something."

They're five feet or so from the edge of the embankment, but otherwise they're effectively in the middle of the yard, and he looks around him as if to say as much.

"Why would they dump it here?"

"Who knows? Maybe they were in a hurry when they left, or maybe by the time they were moving they didn't give a shit anymore. I'll dig it up and toss it over the bank. Tomorrow we can grab a few bags of soil and fill it in, even out the yard back here."

A confused wail floats from the open window at the back of the house, a signal that their window of intimacy is closed.

"Oh fuck, Brody must be up. I'll be right back."

She stands and clears the yard, disappearing back through the screen door.

Clack.

"Sure, don't mind me. I'm right behind you. My ankle's fine," he mumbles, and tries to stand. Pain radiates and spikes from his ankle into his guts, and he collapses back onto the grass, the sand hole inches from his hand. He feels an urge to punch it, to repay it for the violence it inflicted on him, then realizes that would be absurd. Instead, he thrusts his hand into it, expecting the ground under the surface to be cool like it was at the beach when he was a kid, his parents burying him to the neck in the fine sand. Instead, it's warm to the touch and seems to be throbbing, pulsing, but that could be the blood hammering in his temples, his ankle, his heart.

He pulls his hand from the hole and brushes sand from his fingers, picks up the shovel where it lies in the grass. Its blue surface entrances him, and he turns it over in his hands until Melissa remembers he's hurt and comes to help him inside.

3.

MELISSA SETTLES TREVOR on the couch with a blanket and a book, then sets Brody up outside with a portable swing. Its A-frame legs are fitted with a crossbar that is home to a large spring holding a harness that looks to Melissa like a hard-plastic diaper. Brody giggles and spits from inside it, bouncing in the cool grass in the shade of the pine trees.

She glances at him for a moment, taking in the world as he must see it. A new environment, their house, their *home,* and instead of feeling alien and lost, he is embracing it with the innocence of, well, a child. What a wonder it must be to walk new into something without the baggage of lived experience, without all the second-guessing and self-doubt that accompanies prolonged existence on this horrid, spinning rock. She sighs, glances back at the house, breathes in the gratitude she feels, and tries to live in that moment with Brody.

From the shed, Melissa grabs a shovel and a five-gallon bucket then proceeds to fill it with sand from the hole in the yard. The afternoon sun is hot, and before long she pours sweat, the water falling to the sand in dark drops that absorb and disappear. She dumps the bucket down the bank, the sand pushing down ferns and weeds, dribbling slowly toward the release of the river, a vein in the earth on which to float forever. A second bucket joins it, then a third, a fourth, her arms burning from the effort, and her t-shirt soaked with sweat. No matter how far she digs, she doesn't reach soil, but after she's carved a three-foot hole in the yard, she resigns from the chore, confident they can fill the void with soil tomorrow when she goes to Lowe's.

She's about to throw the last bucket—the fifth bucket?—when she realizes she's not holding a bucket at all, is holding Brody, squirming and grunting in her arms. Her feet are at the edge, the point where the incline begins and the slope falls, covered in foliage, to the river below. There is no memory of getting here, holding him like this, but a thought enters her mind, so sudden and unwelcome—what if she did throw him? What if she could dispose of him, launch him down the bank and into the river and send him away, east, gone-to Philadelphia, the harbor, the ocean, the world.

She gasps, falls back—how long was she standing here?—and Brody treats it like a game, thinks he's tackled Mommy, has no idea how close he came to being just another bucketful of sand dashed on the side of the hill. She can't remember picking him up, can't remember stepping to the embankment, but feels confident she was going to throw him. She's never felt malice toward him before, doesn't harbor the well of resentment that she knows boils deep in Trevor. Heat exhaustion, over-exertion, stress. These must have shaken into a terrible cocktail that caused her to pick up her child, carry him to the bank and

throw

think of throwing him. *Fuck.* She wipes sweat from her forehead with a bandana.

Brody totters and she grabs him, continuing the game while inside her mind panics. She looks over to the spot in the yard she's been digging at.

Sand from the sides of the hole cascades down to rest in the bottom, the surface filling slowly like that of an hourglass. She reaches in, scoops a handful of sand, and allows it to drop back in, lets herself become enamored with the natural flow of the grains, thinking how Brody would have followed the sand down the bank to the river, the rapid descent to the bottom.

4

THEY WRAP AND ice his ankle though he insists it's only a sprain. In the evening and through to the next morning, he tries to hide from Melissa that he needs to lean on a chair, a wall, the couch for support, his face twisted in a grimace.

He exists at the crossroads of two worlds, one in which he is thankful for the respite, the time to rest, and another where the anxiety of home improvement projects and the feeling of not pulling his weight in the house crashes over him like a wave.

Yard work falls to Melissa, and now that he's a day into his injury, he is relegated to watching Brody, something about the bank, the river makes Melissa nervous.

His laptop is open on the coffee table, a document full of possible starts for a new product description, but his temples throb in time with his ankle, and he can't concentrate. Melissa knows that he can't work like this, with distractions, with *him,* the tiny monster actually smashing blocks together for no reason other than to hear the clack, a hollow wooden noise to mirror the empty metal one of the screen door.

Clack.

He types a few words, tries to block it out, tries to focus, looks up scowling at Brody.

"Hey, man, you think you could play with something else?"

For the length of Brody's life, Trevor has made no

12

secret that he despises baby talk. At his insistence, he and Melissa speak in full sentences to Brody, no cooing, no slurred words, no raspberries.

In response, Brody picks up two blocks and smashes them together in front of his face, a toy monkey holding cymbals, eyes wide and innocent.

Trevor tries to stand, wants to make it over there, to take those blocks and throw them in the trash, throw them in the yard, bury them in the sand hole, throw them off the bank, throw Brody off the bank, but when he puts weight on his ankle it sits him down and he's there sweating on the couch when the screen door clacks, Melissa standing in the living room looming over him.

"Trevor, are you okay?"

He breathes hard, waves her away.

"The sand worked its way back up again."

"Excuse me?" Brody clacks blocks on the floor, his ankle screams, and the last thing he wants added to his pounding head is nonsense about sand.

"The sand, the hole? Yesterday I shoveled it into buckets and threw it down the bank, but today it doesn't look like I did a damn thing."

"Are you sure you did?"

Something flicks across her eyes, and Trevor regrets this, knows that he's snappy because of his ankle, because of Brody. Was he really thinking of throwing Brody in the river? He shakes his head, like to clear it.

"I'm sorry. I believe you. Today is just annoying already." He rubs his temples, takes a drink of water from a glass on the table. This time when he puts weight on his ankle it holds, but the pain is immense, a dull ache wrapped in a white-hot sear. The pain must show on his face because Melissa walks toward him, starts to say something, but he holds up a hand.

"Let's go check this thing out."

5.

BRODY SITS IN a playpen this time, a base with a two-foot wall of mesh fencing meant to keep him in, meant to keep him from escaping. Keep me from grabbing him as easily, Melissa thinks.

She's embarrassed by the events of the previous afternoon and doesn't tell Trevor, not yet, she'll wait until his ankle feels better, until he can better understand what happened without jumping to conclusions. It must have been heat exhaustion, delirium brought on by the work and the heat, but she's never blacked out before, never lost time like that.

Trevor, despite expressing belief in her story of the buckets of sand she removed, insists on digging for himself, so she fetches the shovel and a garden trowel for him. He digs splayed out on his side like a seal, left arm propping him up and leg jutting useless behind him. When they first discovered it, the hole was barely a foot in diameter, a small patch of sand obscured by grass. Now, they sit around the rim of a growing lesion, a blight in their yard made worse by their digging and scraping.

"I just don't fucking get it," Trevor says, panting.

"I told you, it's crazy, it's like we're not doing anything at all."

Trevor scoops a handful of the sand and lets it fall through his fingers, some of the grains clumping and falling in moist plops. All at once, his mind tingles with the lizard brain instinct that he's being watched, and he looks

14

up to the fence that separates their yard from the Grubers'. Eyes, tiny fingers poking between the slats, then movement flashes between the panels, and a thousand curses and snappy remarks grow in his throat, wither, die.

"Did you meet the neighbors yet?" he asks.

"No, I was planning on going over there tomorrow, taking cookies or something."

He wants to say something about the peeping Tom, about how she should tell them to make sure they respect the privacy of the privacy fence, but she speaks before he can package it in a way that won't sound shitty.

"Trevor, you're bleeding," Melissa says. He looks to his hand like he didn't realize, and she's right, his fingers are stained red, and the sand is clotting around the sticky blood.

"Shit, I must have cut myself on the trowel," he says, uncertain, looking up to her for confirmation. She didn't see him cut himself but that must be it. They're in the yard with nothing else—no sticks, rocks, knives, thorns. She stands.

"C'mon, let's get you cleaned up. You can take a bath and soak your ankle."

She throws his arm around her shoulder and helps him up, noticing that the blood he dripped into the sand is gone, soaked into the ground like it was swallowed.

6.

STEAM RISES LIKE dancing smoke from the tub, the water hot and soothing on Trevor's sore joints. Melissa draws the bath for him and helps to lower him into it, his ankle propped on the lip of the tub. With him safely in the water, she opens a bottom cabinet, the old hinge squeaking in protest, and brings out a bag of epsom salts. She drops a handful into the tub slowly, letting it fall through her fingers like—well, like grains of sand—and sits there on the lip of the tub staring at her hand, mesmerized.

"Miss? You okay?"

"Yeah, it's just—what the hell, Trevor. I can't push this thing away. There has to be an explanation. There just has to be. Did Tammy give us any contact information for the previous homeowner?"

Trevor's teeth itch. The sand is at the forefront of his mind also, but he wants to ease her mind of it, keep her calm. He's decided that she will keep the house together, keep them all afloat, while he investigates further in between work projects. He's already thinking about how to tackle the hole tomorrow when she leaves for work. Mysteries, like this seemingly bottomless pit they've uncovered in their yard, call to him at a base level, ignite his creative impulses and drive his waking hours. He resolves to figure it out, hell or high water.

The pull to the house, the low-level thrum that they both felt when they toured it, is still a presence in his mind, and he notices now, in the tub, that it's increased since they

16

discovered the hole. Not in volume or intensity necessarily, but in a way he can't quite explain, it seems more *there*. Or is it just the throbbing in his ankle, the throbbing that seems to pulse up his leg, through his guts, along his spinal cord, and into his brain? The throbbing that he can't stop focusing on, can't stop imagining words and music over, like it's some sort of grisly drumbeat living in his blood.

Two fingers jab him in the forehead, pulling him from his musing.

"Are you listening to me, Trev? Maybe we should take you to the doctor tomorrow. I can call my dad, and he can—"

"I'm fine, Miss, I promise. I'm going to take it easy tomorrow. I have a light workload. I only have one project on a strict deadline, so I can take time to rest and nap. Make tea."

"Alright," she says, but her tone indicates she is not convinced. "Take it easy, and let's get you up and moving." She cups water in her hands and lets it pour out over his head, wetting the thick dark hair that still draws her to him. "If I keep having to do all the yard work, we're going to need a second tub to soak both our aches."

Her fingers trace his face, down his neck, stop at his shoulder.

"You have a pretty big bruise here," she says, and her fingers trace a pattern, a circle. He cranes his neck, pushes his eyes to the sides of their sockets, but can't quite make out the full scope of it, sees just the edge of a patch of skin growing dark purple and tinged with green, the dark marbling of rich meat circled in mold. "Did you fall on the mower handle or anything when you tripped?"

Trevor doesn't remember falling on the handle and says as much. He raises a hand to feel it for himself. Under the skin, the way a pimple will dwell malicious like a mole, he can feel a mass, a lump, something stewing just beneath the surface. He pushes gently, rubbing in a circular motion to match the one Melissa traced.

Something inside moves around under his fingers. The gritty scrape he feels is not unlike sand.

17

7.

"**TOMMY SAYS Y'ALL** are digging a pretty big hole in the backyard. Hope nothing's wrong with the well pump already."

Frank Gruber is a peach-colored, swollen man, his flesh bulging like an all-over bee sting. By contrast, his wife Liz is thin and stringy, leather stretched taut across overcooked chicken breast. Melissa picks her mug up from their scuffed kitchen table and takes a sip of tea to stall.

"Nah, nothing like that. Just doing some landscaping."

Before she goes over, Trevor tells her about the eyes in the fence, the peeping Tom, and they don't have to agree out loud that the anomaly of the infinite sand hole is something they should keep close to the vest for now. They've just moved in, want to make a go of this, a home, and don't want the neighbors thinking they're looney tunes right off the bat.

Frank nods solemnly, and she can see more questions swirling in his eyes, but he keeps quiet.

Tommy, the ten-year-old peeping Tom, is in the living room showing Brody his action figures. Brody is more interested in trying to remove their various limbs and smashing them into the carpet.

"How are you liking it here so far?" Liz asks. Her voice matches her frame, high-pitched and reedy. She looks nervous, like she's just heard of small talk and is trying it out. "Is your husband working?"

Trevor is at home nursing his ankle, another thing that

18

both of them decided could wait before becoming public knowledge.

"He's working hard on the house. We have a lot of little stuff to catch up on, but we didn't want to be rude, so I wanted to come over and say hello and introduce us, let you know that we've joined the neighborhood."

Frank picks his third cookie from the plate she brought over.

"That's a great house. I was over there a lot when Walter lived there."

"Oh, was Walter the owner before us?"

"Yep," Frank says, crunching cookie onto the tablecloth and earning a stern look from his wife. "Walter Henderson. Used to work downtown at the battery factory. Hell of a fisherman. Always had a beer to share." A wistful glint takes up residency in his eye.

Melissa nearly groans out loud so blunt is the hint. "If you catch Trevor outside, you should pop over. There's a bunch of beer in our fridge, and I know he wants to meet the neighbors also."

Melissa smiles, the thought of Trevor being locked in a conversation with Frank about fishing while being forced to share his beer is too good to not show on her face.

"Why did Walter move out, if you don't mind my asking?"

"Not at all. He's in a nursing home. Got to be so that he couldn't take care of himself anymore, couldn't take care of the property, and his ungrateful kid that lives across the country in Los Angeles"—pronounced Las An-gel-lees—"couldn't be bothered to take him in, so he put him up in the home across town. Pays all his bills and all that on time, way I hear it, but rarely visits. Just doesn't really want to be bothered."

"How's the little one taking to it?" Liz asks, clearly eager to be off of this dour subject.

"Oh, he's taking it okay. You know kids, they're pretty resilient."

JUSTIN LUTZ

"That's why I asked about the well pump, I guess," Frank says, his eyes somewhere else, ignoring the fact that the conversation has moved on without him. "I thought Walter had already replaced it himself. Near the end, before his kid took him away, he spent a lot of time back there digging in the yard."

8.

TREVOR IS STIRRED awake by a cluster of voices outside the window, the faraway slur of drunks leaving a bar. At first, he intends to roll over and ignore it, snatch the tendrils of sleep still shrouding his brain and pull them tight, but then he starts to pick words from the din, and his focus is pulled from sleep by his full bladder. He's asleep on the couch in the living room, choosing to avoid the stairs to the bedroom until he feels a little more comfortable on his ankle. Outside the window, he can see patrons of the All-Weather stumbling to their cars, each chirping and blinking their unlocked blink, welcoming the drinkers to try their best, step inside, take me for a spin. Not for the first time, he wonders if they made a mistake, if this will become a problem, and resolves to call about that fence this week. Dragging his still swollen ankle behind him, he lets the curtain cover the window and tromps his way to the bathroom at the back of the house.

Above the toilet, inexplicably, is a window that looks out onto the backyard. It's the first window they put a curtain on, Melissa thinking it creepy, but Trevor doesn't mind it, deep down somewhere relishes the idea of some strange voyeurism, and always pulls the curtain aside when he takes a piss. Part of this is to admire the backyard, his own twisted way of having gratitude. Another larger part is that he thinks of himself as still part wild, a bit feral, and his suburban way of showing this is marking his yard.

Keeping the curtain pulled aside is a compromise, an indoor marking of the property, a meaningless gesture that he explains to himself as a small homage to his wilder ancestors.

He doesn't turn the bathroom light on, and the only light in the backyard is a feeble glow from the parking lot of the bar, so when something moves across it in the shadows, the lighting change is drastic enough to startle him. He jumps, dick in hand, and is betrayed by his bad ankle yet again. He staggers to the side—spraying the plunger, the toilet brush, and the floor—cursing. When his sweatpants are pulled back up, he presses his face to the glass to get a better look, his mouth fogging the bottom half.

There it is again—a quick movement, but a movement all the same—this time halfway back the yard, splitting the distance to the shed, and he swears it's a figure, a man. Fuck. The last thing he wanted to do tonight was hustle a lost drunk out of his yard, but he stumbles into the kitchen and grabs a flashlight, careful to ease the screen door shut, both to not wake Melissa and Brody and to not scare off his midnight visitor. If a drunk is trespassing in the yard, he wants to take a crack at him himself, wants a moment of confusion where maybe the guy can come at him, take a swing, and Trevor can use the moment to swing the heavy flashlight, that swing weighted with his frustration with the house, Brody, his ankle.

He creeps through the backyard, keeping close to the Grubers' fence to stay hidden in shadows, his flashlight off until he needs it, until he's flanking the intruder, is within stalking, grabbing, hitting distance.

So focused is he on the bulk of the yard, the pockets of shadows under the drooping pine trees and the cover cast by the shed, that he reaches the back of the property without realizing and almost takes a step too far, a step into the nothing hanging beyond the lip of the bank. He pulls his foot back, putting too much pressure on his bad ankle and nearly falling backward onto the yard. Resigning to his lack of stealth, he flicks on the flashlight and does a sweep of the yard.

Nothing.

Carefully, still trying not to startle any trespasser, he creeps around the back of the shed, behind the pines. Still nothing.

In a grim realization, he shines his light down the bank, hoping the drunk didn't take one step too far like he almost did, a step into nothing, and tumble down into the river. He's sure he would have heard the splash and sighs in relief when there's no one there, no one clinging desperately to a sapling, the roots just barely tethering them to the steep drop. He's not sure of the legal ramifications of an intruder slipping, falling, dying on their property, but he's not eager to find out.

Almost disappointed, he shakes his head clear. It must have been a trick of the light, a near somnambulistic illusion painted on the walls of his still sleeping mind. He turns, and his light brushes over the sand pit. The light, rather than illuminating the thing, seems almost to be pulled into it, sucked into the void like a black hole.

Dreaming. He must be dreaming—or at least sleepwalking, not fully awake—because he's sure, here in the backyard under the glow of the flashlight, that the thing is moving, *pulsing*.

In fourth grade while studying animal anatomy, some doctor, some butcher, someone had visited their class and brought with him a pig lung. The students, other than the squeamish ones, took turns passing the lung in gloved hands, popping a straw into the valve and blowing gently to simulate the pig's breathing. It was a grisly exercise for students so young, their small hands sticky and glistening with formaldehyde and viscera, but it's what Trevor thinks of now looking at the steady rise and fall of the surface of the sand.

Breathing, that's the word for it, but it can't be, can't

be alive, can't be anything other than a dumped sandbox, an unused septic tank, anything.

Sleep. He needs sleep. This must be a trick of the light, the midnight hour conspiring with the neon glow of the bar to trick him. He turns to go, to get back in the house, back on the couch, back to sleep, but the flashlight catches something sitting in the grass by the lip of the sand, and he pauses. Half obscured by the grass, the object is pale orange, translucent in the beam of the flashlight. He stoops to pick it up, hears the dull clack of tablets inside.

It's a pill bottle, an orange pharmacy bottle with a white, child-proof lid, half-full. This couldn't have blown in from the bar dumpster, he thinks, and spins it in his hand to read the label: Henderson, Walter. Vicodin.

Walter Henderson. Isn't that the name the neighbors told Melissa, the former owner of the house? Trevor's impression of the man keeps declining, especially now after finding a prescription pill bottle that he apparently left in the yard to get covered in soil, soaked in rain, and sunken into the ground only for him to uncover like some midnight archeologist.

And yet . . .

This couldn't have been here the other day. He would have hit it with the lawn mower, would have noticed it when they were digging in the sand. His rumination is interrupted by a fresh stab of pain, a lightning bolt that connects his ankle to his brain via the electrical wire in his spine. He staggers, blinded by pain, the flashlight dropping out of his hand to land in the center of the sand pit.

Still on, the light dims as the flashlight slowly sinks into the pit like quicksand.

"No, no no," he says, dropping to his knees, one hand still clutching the pill bottle, the other pawing sand out of the pit. The light disappears, and the flashlight is gone, no trace of the glow of the beam or the hard plastic feel of the casing.

GIVE UNTO US

Trevor sits back on his haunches, confused, angry, and disoriented, breathing hard.

Under his shirt, matching the hammering of his heart, the growing bruise pulses.

In the last tendrils of neon glow from the bar, he flips the bottle over to look for an expiration date.

TAMMY ANSWERS HER cell phone on the second ring.

"Hey, Trevor, how's it going?" She sounds nervous, he thinks, and wonders what she thinks he could be calling about.

"Hi Tammy, it's going good, going good, getting a bunch of touch-up work done on the house."

"Oh, that's great. I'll have to swing by and see it when you're done." She pauses, and Trevor dwells in it, lets it stretch the distance between them like warm taffy. "So, Trevor, what can I help you with? Everything okay with the house, I hope?" Again, that nervous intonation.

"Oh, sure, everything's great," Trevor says, and he thinks he can hear her body unclench over the line. "I was just hoping to ask you about something, something in the yard, an . . . anomaly, I guess I'd call it. Was there anything in the packets that you got about something weird in the backyard?"

"Something weird? I think you're going to have to be more specific. Did you find a pet cemetery back there or something?" She chuckles, but there's no humor in it.

He rotates the pill bottle in his hand, one pill lighter than he found it last night.

"No, nothing like that. I was mowing the yard and stepped in a hole, and when we examined it, it turned out to be a bunch of sand in the yard. We initially thought it was the sand mound, you know, for a septic tank, but we're on sewer. I guess I was wondering if it wasn't always on sewer. Maybe that's a recent thing, and there's still a septic tank buried under there?"

"I don't remember seeing anything like that on the sheet," she says, and she's back to normal, *her* normal, a sheen of realtor glaze covering any apprehension she felt a moment ago. "I'll look into the house history and give you a call in a few days, if that works?"

"Oh yeah, that would be great," Trevor says, and they disconnect. He stands holding his phone in one hand, pills in the other, leaning against the counter for support, staring into the black void of the screen.

10.

ALONE, A KING in his castle, Trevor cracks a beer at eleven a.m. and heads for the living room, his makeshift office still set up on the coffee table. He's decided to risk the Vicodin again despite the expiration date being scratched out, and is already walking with more confidence, putting more weight on the bruised ankle. He thinks about moving his work things upstairs to his proper office, the room they set up to share before the mowing, before the pit, then thinks better of it. Going from leaning on things for support straight to using the stairs would be too quick a healing, and Melissa might get suspicious. The Vicodin, he decides, is best left unspoken. She wouldn't approve of the pills, prescribed or otherwise, and he is starting to enjoy the more relaxed version of his life that the injury is providing.

What would he say—he's feeling better because he's taking pills he found in the yard?

Weirder still is the notion he has that the pills aren't happenstance, that they didn't blow in from the trash next door and they weren't there a few days ago when he mowed the lawn.

Unshakeable, but absurd, is the thought that the pills came out of the sand.

Melissa mentioned that Walter Henderson, according to the neighbors, was carted out when he couldn't take care of the property. Unsaid but implied—the subtext glowing between the lines like the neon sign next door—is that he

28

was nuts, Trevor thinks, and still rotating the pills in his hands, he thinks an opioid addiction could be the explanation for that rural diagnosis.

On his computer is an email, edits for a project he sent in yesterday. Nothing that demands immediate attention, so he closes the laptop, takes a slug of beer, and prepares for his real goal of the day: recovering the flashlight from its sandy grave. The Vicodin is already making his blood sing, and the Pabst joins the chorus to belt out a high harmony. He grabs a second can and stuffs it in the back pocket of his jeans before heading outside.

October air chills him through his worn sweatshirt, but the sun warms his face and buoys him through the backyard. Daylight completely changes the mood of the property, and what was menacing and cloaked in shadow the night before now shines in fall glory. At first, he walks right past the sand pit without so much as a glance, mesmerized by the late-morning sun reflecting off the running water of the river below. A blue heron launches from the opposite bank, its flight a languid glide downriver. A flash of color appears in his peripheral, and he waves at a pack of kayakers as they pass by, their boats garish and bright on the dull shine of the river.

So mesmerized is he with the river, the trees, the water, the heron that he doesn't hear the footsteps, doesn't sense anyone there at all until a hand lands on his shoulder, and he jumps so violently he almost sends both of them down the bank.

"Hey-o there, neighbor. Sorry, I didn't mean to startle ya. Just wanted to come over and introduce myself, make your acquaintance and all that."

Trevor settles himself on the bank and turns to find a chubby man in Dockers shorts, boat shoes, and a Shenandoah National Park t-shirt. His brain takes a moment skipping gears before it grabs and puts a name to the man.

"Frank Gruber, yeah? My wife told me all about your family."

What Melissa told him when she came home was that Frank was the pinkest man she'd ever seen, as if his blood was trying to escape the prison of his body and was pushing up against his epidermis from the inside. She'd also said that his wife, not present, was like a taxidermied praying mantis that someone accidentally put mammal skin on. He suppresses a laugh, is reminded, like most days, that that cutting humor is part of why they work so well together, why he loves her. Spoken to the Grubers, those words would surely sever any tenuous relationship they were building, but between them, they are a sort of love language.

Frank Gruber beams, the simple act of being recognized boosting his dopamine levels.

"Sure am, and that must make you Trevor, then. Your wife told me all about you as well."

They shake, each worried that the moment the shake breaks they'll have nothing to say, but it's Frank that breaches the awkward sea, paddling a dinghy across with the shoddiest of verbal oars.

"River sure is high, huh? Rain really got her swollen up. Our view isn't quite as spectacular." He gestures next door to their property, as if Trevor could see their bank through the wooden fence. Trevor smiles, thinks about when they lived in the apartment, when he lived in the bustle, how this kind of folksy, rural nonsense would boil his blood, would remind him of all the things he wasn't doing while Frank was bombarding him with this meaningless prattle. They've only been living on Hollenbach Road for just shy of a month, but Trevor thinks he can feel his blood pressure lowering already, the trees, the river, the air smoothing out the rough edges of his anxious, frantic tendencies.

"I love having it back here," Trevor says, then remembering what Melissa said about Frank knowing Walter Henderson, dances around what he really wants to ask. "Walter never tried to put in steps, a dock, anything? I was feeling the call of the river the moment we saw the place."

Trevor takes a swig of his beer, notices Frank's hungry eyes and hands him the one in his back pocket.

Frank nods his thanks like this is some rural quid-pro-quo and takes a drink.

"Nah, when Walter moved in here, he was already in his late sixties. I don't think there were any kind of big construction projects in store for him."

Trevor thinks of what Melissa said about how Frank thought Walter replaced the well pump himself, and shelves it.

"How long have you lived here, Frank?"

"Oh, me and Liz have been here about ten years or so, moved in when she caught pregnant, knew we'd need more room." He offers Trevor a conspiratorial wink. "Well, you know, you've got the little guy. I'm sure that this house was a similar idea for you and Melissa, yeah?"

"Sure, yeah, it definitely was. Our apartment was closing in around us. It was time to upgrade."

Frank nods to the bar on the other side of the property. "You been over to the bar yet? Their wing night is Wednesdays, and they fry a mean cod filet."

They both pause to admire the waft of today's upcoming menu that drifts to them on the breeze: onions and fryer oil.

"Nah, not yet, been breaking in the new kitchen. Do you ever have problems with the bar?"

Frank's face bunches. "Problems? Afraid I'm not sure what you mean."

"Last night, I had to get up to pee," he raises his beer, Frank clanks his can to it in understanding, "and I thought I saw someone in the backyard. Thought maybe a drunk from next door couldn't find his car and wandered in."

"Well, I suppose that'll happen. I think Walter had to chase a drunk or two out of the yard but not often. He said to me a few times that he saw things in the shadows back by the shed. Guess that must be what they were."

31

This thread chills Trevor, but he doesn't pull on it. He takes a sip of his beer to stall, launches into it.

"Was Walter on any kind of pain meds, Frank?"

Frank tips his head like a dog that doesn't understand a command.

"That's a peculiar thing to ask. What brings you to that?"

Trevor shrugs, his lie locked and loaded. "I found a bottle of pills hanging around in a medicine cabinet upstairs. They were expired, and I flushed them, of course. Guess I just wanted to know if there was anything else left in the house that I should look out for, you know," sip, no eye contact, "because of Brody."

If Frank thinks Trevor is lying, he doesn't show it. "Ah, yeah, makes sense. Guess maybe Walt's good-for-nothing kid missed those in his rush to shovel his dad off to the home. Walter didn't keep guns or drugs or anything, if that's the path you're on," he says. He contemplates the river for a beat, drains his can. "Matter of fact, though, I do remember him taking something. He threw out his back, digging to put in the new well pump, or whatever he was doing back here."

Almost like they rehearsed it, the two men turn to the sand pit, dormant in the late morning sun. Trevor wills it to pulse, to beat like a heart, something, anything to show that he didn't dream it, didn't make it up, isn't losing his goddamn mind, but nothing happens. They just stare at it, like waiting for a dog to sit, stay, roll over.

"Say, did you drop this out here?" Frank crouches, his shape not built for bending at the waist, and comes up with something old and crusted in dirt in his hand. He drops his can to the grass and wipes the soil from the object.

In his hand is a knife, the hilted blade maybe four inches long in a leather sheath.

"No, I don't think I did," Trevor says, but his mind is already on overdrive, wondering how yet another strange item appeared in the yard, materializing from nothing as if pulled up out of the ground. Did Walter Henderson go nuts and bury all of his remaining possessions back here? Was he hiding things from his son? Squirreling them away for safekeeping?

Even as he's thinking this, Trevor knows it's wrong, knows with weird certainty that something else altogether is true, that this knife came out of the sand pit, that this knife is an offering, is the offered trade for the flashlight he sent into the sand last night.

He's not sure how he knows this but is sure that he does, the certainty glowing white-hot in his brain, the picture crystal clear.

"It's old, for sure," Frank says, and pulls the blade from the sheath with some effort, "but I think with a little bit of clean up this thing will be a heck of a knife. They don't make shit like they used to, huh?"

Frank admires the knife in the sun, the blade rust-speckled and tarnished but resilient-looking underneath. He hands the knife and sheath to Trevor, to examine, to have, resigning it to the property's rightful owner. Trevor takes the weapon, the handle carved out of deer antler and the sheath patterned with ornate markings. When the handle touches his fingers, it's like electricity, and a vision clouds his brain—him shoving the knife into Frank's stomach and twisting, turning, stirring his guts with the rusted blade. He's opening Frank up like he would field-dress a deer, pulling the gory ropes of his insides out to fall on the sand pit, and the hole is sucking, slurping, swallowing—its greedy mouth pulling everything from Frank and disappearing it into the earth.

Thundering in his temples, his brain, his blood,

kill, gut, rend, destroy, give.

"Trevor, you alright, man?"

He shakes from his nightmare, his grip on the antler handle of the knife enough to whiten his knuckles.

"Sure, yeah, got lost for a second there. I think this will clean up nice. I'll look up how to take the rust off of there."

Frank smiles, but his eyes are distrustful.

"Sure man. I think that'll look great."

Both their eyes fix on the sand anomaly, unsure of what happens now, what's next in the natural order of new neighbor friendships.

"Say, can I have another beer?"

11.

MELISSA RETURNS TO work after two weeks off for settlement, move-in, and Trevor's injury. She wakes early to accommodate the added distance from their new house, mapping a new route to Brody's daycare that takes mostly backroads.

Halfway through the day, the great wheel of time scraping against her in a slow grind, wearing her down to dust, Heather finds her in the break room and traps her by the coffee maker.

"Miss! Hey, I heard you were back today!"

Melissa smiles her plastered-on work smile and nods. She spreads her arms wide in a welcoming gesture. "Here I am, back at last."

While she doesn't mind working at the agency overall, each weekend she has to pull herself up and out of the comforting molasses of time off, personal project time, to prepare once again to sell her time at a loss on Monday morning. The time off to settle into the new house was a welcome break, and the reintegration to the grinding monotony of accounting has left her more drained of life than usual.

Heather brushes past to butt in front of her at the coffee pot.

"How do you like the new house? How much further of a drive is it?"

Melissa's drive has extended by exactly seventeen minutes. She rehearsed this in the car, is ready for the mindless barrage of standard questions that she'll encounter today.

"Oh, it's not too much further. Not bad at all. And it's all backroads." She clutches her empty coffee mug, willing Heather to move, step aside, get the fuck out of the way, so she can escape this hell she's found herself trapped in. "And we love the house," she says, the unspoken "but" a glaring omission. Heather raises an eyebrow, and Melissa sees it. "No, really, we love it. There's just more renovations to do than we initially thought." *And a bottomless pit in our backyard,* she thinks but doesn't say, *a quicksand morass that neither of us can explain.*

At home, she's done her best to avoid thinking about the hole, but she can tell that it fills Trevor's waking thoughts and maybe his dreams, too. She wonders how much he's worked today, whether he's spent the day instead thinking about their lawn anomaly, planning ways of attack, figuring out what's next in his haphazard scientific method.

Mercifully, Heather moves from in front of the coffee maker, and Melissa fills her cup, her conversational safety net. She blows on the top, takes a sip.

"Has Trevor been doing the repairs himself?" Heather asks.

"Yeah, it's not major stuff—patching walls, touching up paint, that kind of stuff. He wants to build a floating dock and a set of stairs down to the river, but I think he's doing all the little, easy stuff first to appease me."

Trevor seems to be recovering at least, this morning walking past her with barely a limp, putting weight back on the ankle, so Melissa holds hope that the repairs can resume in earnest.

Heather's eyes go wide. "You're that close to a river? Is there a fence or anything, or can you just jump in? Like, is it yours?"

Melissa, thinking of the roll of fencing leaning against the shed, makes a mental note to have Trevor move that up the list.

"I don't think it's technically ours, but I think Trevor is using eminent domain on the chunk of the bank that hits our house." She laughs, partly at Trevor's wiles and partly at Heather's empty face at her use of the phrase "eminent domain."

"There's not a fence yet, but it's the first thing I have on the list for when Trevor's feeling better."

Heather scrunches her face, and Melissa could punch herself because there it is, the slip she promised she wouldn't make, the gate creaking open into the courtyard of their personal life, and now she would have to explain the ankle, the yard, the hole that won't go away.

"What's wrong with Trevor? Nothing serious, I hope?" Heather's face is all concern, but Melissa can see a slight curl to her lips, not full malice but a tinge of joy at the idea of someone other than her suffering.

"Oh no, he twisted his ankle the other day mowing the lawn, but he should be back up and running in no time. He was walking pretty well this morning." His mystery bruise jumps into her mind uninvited, and she wonders if that too is passing.

She chambers a lie, pulls the trigger. "Our backyard is so full of chipmunk holes, I think he stepped right into a lair." Her attempt at frivolity dies when she thinks of the real hole, realizing for the first time that its perimeter is the only place in the yard the chipmunks aren't digging. She shudders, sips her coffee.

"You can get smoke bombs for that, you know," Heather says, and Melissa hears her but isn't thinking of the chipmunk holes. "You just drop one deep in there, and it kills whatever's living inside."

12.

BRODY'S DAYCARE IS a squat, brick building outside their old suburb, a structure that always reminds Melissa of a rec building she used to see bands play at in her teens. Inside, the vibe is much the same, a running, teeming mass of young people, this time with more supervision. She pulls up, and Brody and Fae Davenport are waiting outside, Brody's small backpack in her hand and Brody clutching a plastic dinosaur to his chest.

"Ah, Fae, I'm sorry I'm late. Still getting the hang of the new routine," Melissa says. She gets out, rounds the car, and opens the back door for Brody to climb into his car seat.

"Oh, no problem at all. None at all. I'm usually here a little late anyway." She ruffles Brody's hair with her free hand and guides him toward the car. "Plus it gave Brody a little extra time in the sandbox, didn't it, little guy?"

Melissa straightens, air escaping her lungs. "Sorry, what?"

"Oh, Brody found a new favorite place today," she says, handing Melissa the backpack. "He spent all of our outside time today in the sandbox, digging a hole like he was tunneling to China."

13.

BY THE TIME Melissa and Brody park outside the house, the sun is dipping low in the sky, throwing bands of October orange over the backyard in great swaths. Shaken, she feels she must be overreacting, but the whole way home she finds it hard to look at Brody, hard to catch his eyes in the rear-view mirror. It's nothing, it's nothing. He must have been paying more attention than she thought that day, the day she filled bucket after bucket with sand, and the pit didn't get any smaller. The day she threw bucket after bucket of sand down the bank. The day she picked him up and almost made him join it. He must be mimicking her movements, digging like Mommy, digging and digging with no clear purpose and no evident progress.

She wonders, hopes, he won't remember that, or that the sentiment won't be something that sticks with him as he grows. She can't remember anything from when she was two, so why should he? Yes, but, she tells herself, didn't she read in all those parenting books that a vibe is more important than concrete memories? That the spirit in which a child is reared will help determine his temperament? This makes her think of Trevor, who she knows openly resents Brody, and she shudders.

Melissa didn't want to have kids either, never felt any great cosmic pull toward motherhood, but when her urine came out positive, she wasn't upset about it, not like Trevor. She's always felt more comfortable trying to be content in the moment, going with the flow, and letting the universe dictate which forks in the path she takes rather than forcing its hand. If she's having a baby, getting married, buying a house, moving to the country, digging in a bottomless pit of quicksand in the backyard, then that's what she's doing.

Brody squirms in his car seat, trying in vain to undo his own buckle.

"Hold on, buddy, I got you, I got you." She scoops him out, backpack in hand, and behind her hears the slow crunch of tires on gravel.

"Hey there, new neighbor!"

Melissa turns and is greeted by a middle-aged woman leaning out the window of her blue minivan, her hair piled high on top of her head like an erratic beehive. Cat-eye glasses hang from a chain around her neck, and Melissa has no problem imagining them framing the woman's smiling, ruddy face, a garish fifties caricature dropped into rural Pennsylvania. The bumper of the van seems to be held in place by a decoupage of stickers: No Farms, No Food; My Other Car is A Greenhouse; Gardeners for Jill Stein.

"I'm Fran. I live just down there!" Fran points to a house Melissa had noticed but not examined, the structure homologous to the rest of the block but the yard overflowing with plants, practically vomiting them over the fence into the street.

Melissa walks into the road, Brody in one arm, and shakes Fran's extended hand. "I'm Melissa Davis. This is Brody."

"Hi Brody," Fran says, her face split in a wide grin. "Gee, that sure is a cool dinosaur." Brody buries his face in his arm, hiding both his face and the face of the t-rex he still clutches.

"I'm sorry, he's pretty shy—still adjusting to the move, his routine being upended, all that," Melissa says.

"No need to explain, dear," Fran says. She waves a

hand to indicate the rest of her body that Melissa can't see behind the van door. "I've always been a little much for children, I guess." Traffic is starting to line up behind Fran's minivan, not yet honking, but the two drivers behind her look increasingly impatient.

"Look, dear, I wanted to stop you because I'm having a garden party on Saturday." Melissa's face twitches sour and Fran continues. "Not like a stuffy garden party, nothing formal or anything. I'll have food and veritable gallons of wine. It's for the block, I do it every year and all the neighbors come. We'd love to get you in on the tradition early if you're free."

"Oh, that sounds lovely," Melissa says, and means it, yearns to feel more included, connected to the neighborhood. "I'll ask my husband, Trevor, but I'm sure we can stop by."

"Bring a cooler, if you drink anything specific, but like I said, I'll have a ton of wine, and usually when the party winds down Nick or Daphne pops back to their house for a bottle of bourbon." She winks, notices something beyond Melissa's shoulder. "Hi, Mr. Davis! I'll see you Saturday!" More quietly to Melissa, she says, "There, I asked him for you," and winks that conspiratorial wink again. The car behind Fran finally gives in to temptation and honks a short honk. Fran waves and begins to ease her van forward. "And bring the little one. The others bring their kids. See you soon!"

Melissa watches the van crawl down the street, the drum major setting pace in a second line parade, and turn into the gravel drive beside a fence overgrown with vines and flowers. She turns to retreat to the house, and like she expects, Trevor is there on the porch, beer in hand, slightly cocked so as not to put pressure on the ankle that may or may not still be hurting him.

"Who was that? And what does she mean she'll see me Saturday?" His eyes are just barely rimmed in red, and Melissa thinks that he might be half useless this evening—

wonders what he got done today, how much time he spent digging, drinking, staring into the hole in the backyard.

"That's Fran. She lives down the block. The plant house."

"The house with the wild yard?"

That's the pot calling the kettle black, she thinks but doesn't say. "Are you feeling any better?"

He drains his can, crumples it slightly, something they've both always done to signal that the drink is over. "Oh yeah, feeling much better," he says and bounces lightly back and forth, but she can see the wince, see the awkward cant that isn't quite balanced.

"Alright Seabiscuit, no dressage for you quite yet," she says.

"Seabiscuit was a racing horse, not a dancing horse," he says, cracking another beer that appears from the back pocket of his jeans.

In the sweep of the movement, she catches a hint of something new at his hip.

"What's that thing?" She puts Brody down, her arm growing tired, and he plops on the deck of the porch to tromp his dinosaur around their feet.

"Oh, right, I found this," he says, and unsnaps the catch on a leather holster—sheath? She finds she doesn't know the name for a knife holder—and produces a bone-handled hunting knife, the blade gleaming and grisly.

She shudders, hopes it's not visible. She's always detested weapons, and counts her blessings that at least it's not a pistol.

"Found it? Like in the house?"

"Yeah, it was at the back of one of the old cabinets in Brody's room. It was in pretty rough shape, but I cleaned it up, and now it's good as new."

"Brody's room?" She almost shudders again, can't help herself, thinks of her toddler finding a rusted old hunting knife and wielding it like a dirty sword. "Let's hope there's no other weird dangerous shit hidden around the house."

"Nah, this is it, at least as far as I could find," he says. "I did a sweep after I found the knife, knocked on panels, floorboards, looking for secret compartments." He's smiling now, his winning smile, his everything-is-fine-you-can-trust-me smile, the one that wins her over day after day, and she'll be damned if she doesn't trust him, if she doesn't think that despite the new house and its seemingly endless repairs, despite hidden knives in the walls, despite the quicksand in the yard, things really will all be okay.

"So, what," she says, scooping up Brody and pushing past Trevor to enter the house, "you're a knife guy now? You'll stab your eye out, you know."

He laughs and follows her inside. "I was in the Boy Scouts. I have my Tote 'n Chip."

The laughter follows them inside, the tiny lies swirling around Trevor's head like mayflies in summer heat.

MELISSA ROLLS OVER, her arm searching for Trevor in the dark only to find that his side of the bed is cold. Her brain first puts him on the couch, his ankle keeping him from taking the stairs, then the blocks click into place, and she remembers his recovery. On the bedside table, the neon numbers of the alarm clock blast light into her eyes that declares it's three a.m.

Swinging her legs out of bed, she is mindful of every board, every creak and groan of the house. The last thing she wants to do is wake Brody and restart the cycle of stories, milk, exhaustion. She pads to the stairs in her bare feet with a full bladder, the hardwood cool underfoot. In the bathroom, she stands from the toilet, and when she turns to flush it, the glow of the bar sign throws shadows into the yard, and she catches something, a figure, sitting in the grass at the rear of the property.

Trevor.

Careful, careful with the screen door, the metal begging to spring from her hand, to whap into the frame and announce its presence to the neighborhood, she creeps from the house and onto the side porch, the concrete cold and harsh on her feet until she gets to the cool relief of the grass.

Getting closer, she can pick out more details, her husband sitting cross-legged next to the hole, the sand pit, the bottomless *thing* in their yard. Something reflects the light, catches it and bounces it back in a garish refraction, and she sees the beer can raised to his lips, lowered, raised, drained, crushed, tossed to join the others that litter the ground around him. When he cracks a fresh one, the sound makes her jump, so sudden is it in the relative quiet, but he still doesn't show signs of noticing her approach.

Behind him, she runs a hand through his hair and he only flinches a little, seems to know she was there, maybe she was there all along.

"I put a beer in it," he says, his eyes never leaving the sand, the sand static and unmoving in the light of the moon, the far-off neon glow. "To see what comes out."

She nods and all at once she has an answer to a question she didn't ask, hadn't been thinking of. An understanding enters her brain as if placed there, an understanding that the knife she noticed Trevor wearing last night is from the sand, birthed out of the yard like a gift.

What will be given in return, she doesn't know, but something eases into her brain and cradles it, tells her it doesn't matter, it never mattered. Fog fills her head, and she shakes it, but the haze won't clear, so she embraces it instead, leans into it like a thick blanket. Her hand caresses his hair and moves down to rub his neck, his shoulders.

Under his shirt, her hand brushes something, a lump, and when he winces she has time to think that it's the same spot she saw the bruise the other night, the night in the tub, and was that a wince or a shudder? She grazes it again, her fingers dancing gently around it over his shirt, and she notices that the fabric is beginning to moisten, something thick and wet seeping through the cotton of his sleep t-shirt. This time it's definitely a shudder not a wince, and a small gasp escapes his mouth when her fingers find the center of the spot and gently push.

Without asking, she kneels in the grass behind him and bunches the hem of his shirt in her hands, his arms lifting in compliance when she lifts the shirt over his head.

This time it's her who gasps.

On his shoulder, the bruise has grown, opened, split, and is now a sore, a wound, a hole in his shoulder seeping thick, yellow liquid and rising with his breathing as if tasting the air. Trickling down his skin to land on the ground is a fine powder, something gritty that with a touch she confirms is sand. On his torso are more bruises, more like what the shoulder thing used to be, started out as. Green and purple splotches that dot the sky of his chest and stomach like grisly constellations.

"Oh Trevor, what is happening," she asks, but she finds she doesn't mean it, her words hanging in the air as though placed in molasses. Her fingers find his shoulder again, find the sore, dance around the edges and gently prod the center, the slick pus allowing her digit entrance. This time he doesn't gasp, he moans, and she can feel on the tip of her finger a light pressure, a gentle suckling like a calf on a teat, and she wants to be repulsed, but her mind fills with warmth and color and light so she gives her finger more pressure, entering him further, and he's panting, the walls of the sore warm and pushing against her finger like to hold it inside.

From her kneeling position she reaches around his belly to his crotch and finds that he's fully erect, the gorge of his cock pulling taut the thin fabric of his pajama pants. She shuffles around him, her knees in the sand now, her finger still inserted in his shoulder wound. When she pulls it out, it's slick with pus, and she puts it in her mouth, the taste like salt and dirt and blood. The finger comes out clean, and she kisses Trevor with a mouth still full of him, the yellow discharge passing between their mouths and dripping down his chin.

He guides her t-shirt over her head, and she pushes the elastic of his pajama pants down his hips, both rocking to their knees to aid in the disrobe. She pushes him gently, and he lies down in the yard, the sand cool against the skin of his back. Under them, she feels the earth give then push back, knows that the pit is pulsing like his wound, sucking at the air as if gasping, breathing, calling.

GIVE UNTO US

Straddling him, she works to guide him inside, and he stops her, takes her hand, and presses it to his chest. Some of the bruises have swollen, popped, are oozing their discharge onto his skin, and she presses her palm into it like finger painting before grabbing his erection, painting it slick with the pus, and sitting down on it.

They rock that way in the cool night air, slick with the juices of him.

Beneath them, the sand pulses in time with their carnal rhythm.

15

WITH NO SIDEWALK to connect their block, Trevor's rolling cooler bounces and grinds in the chip of the road, Melissa leading the way, coaxing an already tired and grumpy Brody. She's grumpy herself, her body sore, a vague memory of late-night sex floating in the back of her brain. Trevor has been known to wake wanting it, groping at her half-asleep in the dark, but she can usually remember those occasions and usually doesn't wake with a bruise growing on the inside of her thigh. She noticed it while getting dressed and traced it with her finger, a fog settling over her mind when she pondered its origin. She passed it off as new house jitters, breaking in the new bed.

This trek to Fran's is the first time they walk the neighborhood since moving in, the first time they get a good look up close at the other houses they share the block with.

"I'm glad we got the house we did," Trevor says, a little bit of both gratitude and judgment in his voice. No cars pass during their walk, and they stroll cavalier down the center of the eastbound lane. Melissa keeps a close eye on Brody, creating a buffer between him and the center of the road with her body so as to shove him to the shoulder in the event a roaring car materializes around the bend down the way.

Two houses away from Fran's, they can hear music, the thump of a soulful bass line resonating in Trevor's chest, and he allows himself to think that this might not be so bad. He's stocked his rolling cooler with Pabst, and Melissa said that the Fran woman implied there would be bourbon if he stuck it out long enough, so that was reason enough to give the party a go. He also genuinely does want to meet his neighbors, less for a sense of community like Melissa and more just to know the people he lives amongst. His first taste of neighborly life has been a mixed bag as he finds Frank Gruber nice enough but thinks him a nosy mooch, a guy who came next-door mostly to check up on Trevor and try to liberate him of his beers.

In the back of his mind is the pit, pulling at him like tiny threads willing him to return to his house. Loading the cooler that morning, cold cans sweating in his hand, he had a fading memory of feeding a beer can to the pit in the middle of the night, and if he did so, he wants to see what comes out, figure out the exchange rate. He has a similar foggy memory of taking Melissa last night, and the strained way she walks ahead of him confirms it. He smiles with wolfish pride.

He's seen Fran's house from down the block and from the inside of the car driving past, but to see it up close is an altogether different thing. There's a fence out front, but his knowledge of it stops there. No color or material is visible under the thick blanket of kudzu, and on first blush, it would easily fool anyone into thinking it's not a fence at all but a very thin hedge. A narrow concrete walkway leads to a porch painted in garish purples and blues, nearly every surface occupied with a potted plant or concrete sculpture. Gnomes peek out of flower pots, carved squirrels hang from wooden posts. More plants create a walkway that leads around the side of the house, and they walk down a leafy, green corridor past a recycling bin and multiple compost containers.

The corridor opens onto Fran's backyard, and they step into a different world. Raised-bed garden boxes segment the back of the yard, and the rear fence is a mirror of the front, though twice as high. Bamboo stalks border the rear, and potted plants are everywhere. What first looks like a haphazard mess is revealed on closer inspection to be a well-ordered explosion, types of plants corresponding to their individual light, soil, and water needs. The thing that seems out of place is the presence of people, neighbors lounging in folding chairs holding wine glasses and talking, a group of small children playing hide-and-seek between the garden boxes.

"Ah, you made it!" Fran materializes from the house holding a plate of cheese and meat cubes, a sweating bottle of rosé cradled under each arm. "Let me just get rid of all this, and I can show you around. Put your cooler over there on Cooler Row, Mr. Davis. Can I get any of you anything?"

"Trevor, please," he says, reaches a hand to shake, settles for a bumped elbow.

Trevor lines his cooler up with a series of them and reaches inside for a beer. Brody tugs at Melissa's hand, and she lets go of it, letting him run on pudgy legs to the backyard with the other children.

"Don't worry about him, all the neighbor kids are nice," Fran says, placing a glass of wine in Melissa's hand. "They're like our little free-labor babysitters on days like this. And don't worry," she adds, seeing the distant look toward the back of the yard, the concerned look in Melissa's eyes, "we don't have river access here quite like you do. Our bank is a mess of cinder blocks and big rocks, and I've got the whole thing fenced off and the gate locked, anyway. C'mon, let me show you the house, get you acquainted!"

Fran leads Melissa toward the house, and she waves a half-hearted wave toward Trevor who salutes her with his newly-cracked beer and drinks the foam off the top of it. He scans the yard, debates just hanging by himself, isolating and observing rather than talking to anyone, and then Frank Gruber finds his eyes from across the party and launches across the yard like a scud missile.

"Hey there, Trevor! Glad you could make it," Frank says. Trevor notices that, mercifully, he has his own beer in hand already, and holds out his to cheers. "Did you just get here?"

"A moment ago, yeah. Fran already absconded with Miss," Trevor says. He points with his beer can to the back of the yard where the children are running through the garden boxes, Brody tottering behind smiling and laughing. "And Brody has already left me to join the wild rumpus."

Frank laughs, but Trevor can tell he doesn't get the reference. This, Trevor decides in the moment, might be the reason he doesn't like Frank and the reason he finds it so hard to connect to people in general. The disconnect between honesty and public performance, the urge to laugh when you don't get the joke.

Trevor drains his beer and pulls another from the cooler in a rattle of ice.

"Have you met anyone else on the block yet, or am I the lucky one?" Frank asks, and Trevor's blank eyes as he cracks the tab are answer enough. "C'mon, I'll introduce you around, make you Mr. Neighborhood."

Trevor follows Frank to the nearest group of people, wonders if when he sees them he'll be able to associate each set of neighbors to their house on sight alone, resolves to try. A circle of canvas camping chairs sags under the weight of pale meat stuffed into ratty jeans and work boots. *This is the confederate flag house,* Trevor thinks, and when one of them leans forward to refresh his drink, it reveals a "Don't Tread On Me" pattern woven into the folding chair.

Trevor puts a tick on his mental score-card.

"Hey, gang, did you meet your new neighbor yet?" Frank asks, sliding into their conversation without waiting for a lull. "Trevor and his family moved into Walt's place next door."

There are mumbles of recognition, and Don't Tread On Me stands up to shake Trevor's hand, wipes it on his jeans like to clean it.

"Good to meet you, Trevor." The grip is meaty and strong, and Trevor wants to wince but doesn't. "I'm George, George Dent. This is my wife, Patty." Patty doesn't stand, raises a wine glass like a toast, drains it. "We live two down."

In the Confederate Flag House, Trevor thinks but doesn't say, giving it proper noun status in his mind. He scrunches his eyes like fitting mental blocks into place, nods solemnly, all of it a show, all of it his public-facing performance.

He feels a pulse in his ankle and resists the urge to look back to their house, to the hole, to bolt, to run to it. Absent-mindedly, he touches his shoulder, grazes the lesion growing there that's sealed back to a bruise.

"I'm still putting everybody in their houses, assembling the street as I meet people, you know?" Trevor says.

If this is a weird way of putting it, George doesn't show it. He introduces Trevor around their circle of camping chairs—the couple who live next to them, a gaggle of kids whose names Trevor can't be bothered to remember.

"How are you liking the block so far, Trevor?" One of the women, Daphne Wyngard, wife of Horace, asks.

Trevor thinks of their years in the apartment—how the neighbors in the downstairs unit came and went so quickly he didn't get to know any of them, how he mostly stayed cooped up inside even before Brody came and shackled him to the parental wall of the place, thinks how this is what he wanted, a community, a small town—and smiles at Patty.

"We love it here. It's quiet. Everyone is nice so far." He goes out on a limb, offers Frank's shoulder a playful slug. "Y'know, except for this guy showing up immediately to suck down my beer."

Trevor thinks he sees Frank wince and instantly regrets this, but the regret is swallowed by George Dent and Horace Wyngard's deep belly laughs.

"Ah, shit, he's going to fit in pretty well, yeah?"

"Yeah Frank, do you even know where the beer distributor is?"

Frank flushes red but plays along, slugs Trevor back, a little harder than playful.

"Yeah, yeah, alright guys. Sorry I'm good company." Frank glances around the yard. "Want to keep making the rounds, Trevor?"

Trevor waves goodbye to the chair circle amidst a chorus of come-over-any-time and the-beer-fridge-is-always-full. He knows he won't take them up on this, but it feels good to be invited. He does a cursory sweep for Melissa and, not finding her, repeats the sweep to locate Brody, sees him still running through the planter boxes.

Frank leads him back to Cooler Row, and they freshen their drinks.

"I like those guys enough," he confesses about the Wyngards, the Dents, "but they fuckin' rib me every chance they get." He cracks his beer and takes a healthy slug. "I can take it as good as the next guy, but they don't let up."

Trevor almost feels bad for him, his lack of self-awareness and genuine desire to just be accepted at the adult version of the cool kids table. He wonders if, given enough time, he'll feel that way, or if he'll be content with his wife, his son, his unfillable hole.

"Frank, how's it hanging, young man?"

An older man sidles up next to Frank, leans to take a beer out of an antique looking Coleman cooler plastered with bumper stickers from small town bars—The Belly Up, Smokey's.

"Hey, Nick, we were working our way around the party. I've been introducing everyone to Trevor. He bought Walt's place."

Nick Harper stands with his beer, a sweating bottle that he cracks with an opener attached to his keys on a carabiner at his hip. He's shorter than Trevor but projects as taller, an untucked flannel shirt opened a few buttons at the neck and rolled at the sleeves to reveal the hints of a body blanketed in tattoos—swallows, naked women, nautical stars—brandings that Trevor can identify as meaningful but doesn't know the significance of. His salt and pepper hair is high and tight, his mustache full grey.

For what feels like the fortieth time today, Trevor takes an offered hand and shakes. Nick's grip is firm and lingers, a steady squeeze accentuated by the carpet of grey hair on the back of his hand. Hands break apart, bottle meets can, and they drink to the introduction.

Nick doesn't say much else, and Trevor appreciates this about him immediately. Where Frank feels the need to fill any available silence with prattle, almost like it makes him nervous, Nick stands instead in the calm silence at the edge of the throbbing party.

A shout of "Dad!" erupts from the garden boxes at the back of the yard and a half-dozen heads turn and then resume their conversation when they realize it's not their boy who's called. Tommy approaches across the yard, shouting for Frank, and holds his hand in the air above his head, the palm slowly filling with blood.

"Ah, shit, fellas. Seems like I've got to take care of this." Frank tries to speak calmly, but the blood rushes out of his face. "Talk amongst yourselves."

Trevor and Nick watch him take long strides across the yard, scoop Tommy from behind and shepherd him into the house, asking him what happened in hushed tones. Once more, almost like an afterthought, Trevor scans the yard for Brody, sees no change in his behavior or demeanor, and feels content enough to leave him be.

"Nice enough guy," Trevor says.

"He's a mooch and a dolt. Means well. Tries too goddamn hard."

They cheers again, and a few moments stretch to minutes and pass just like that, the crisp autumn day keeping good company.

"So, what was the cost of that knife, Trevor?"

Trevor's hand goes to the sheath at his belt instinctively, though he's had enough beers to almost forget he was wearing it at all. Melissa thinks he should leave it at home, feels a visible weapon only invites trouble, but since cleaning it, Trevor can't imagine being without it, feels a void when it's not strapped to his belt. Though it's absurd, and he can't explain it, he almost feels as though he's earned it, that it's some prize he deserves for perseverance and triumph of will.

"Sorry?" So strangely phrased is the question that he stumbles and isn't sure what to say, the cogs of available lies not fitting into place quickly enough to exit his mouth in a way that seems believable.

"The knife. Looks nice. Was wondering the cost." Nick asks this without turning his head to look at Trevor, the longneck sweating in his meaty hand.

"Oh, I don't remember. Couldn't have been more than twenty dollars or so."

Nick still doesn't look at him, waits a beat before he replies. "That's the price. I was wondering about the *cost*."

"I don't think I know what you—"

Now Nick does turn to look at him. His voice doesn't rise in volume, but the intensity in his eyes pins Trevor to the spot.

"I think you do, man. I've lived here a long time, and I recognize that knife. I know it belonged to Walter Henderson, and I know that because I sold it to him." He drains his bottle and drops it to the grass, fishes another from his cooler without taking his eyes from Trevor. "So I'll ask you one more time, for your own sake, and if you want to keep pretending, that's fine, but then I won't help you. Though maybe," he looks Trevor up and down like examining him, locks on his shoulder, the damp spot that Trevor can now feel there, "you're beyond help already. So, one more time. What was the cost?"

Trevor weighs this in his mind, takes in everything about this strange and thrumming man and decides he already knows more than he's willing to say, takes a chance.

"A flashlight."

Nick nods, resumes his former stance looking out over the yard.

"By accident or on purpose?"

"A little bit of both," Trevor says, remembering the half-hearted way he dug for the light, the fascination in watching it sink and imagining the beam illuminating some subterranean world.

"Anything else?"

"What do you mean?"

Nick sighs, his eyes softening and his voice losing its edge in favor of sympathy. "Did you give it anything else?"

Trevor has understood, maybe without sound logic, but with abject certainty, that the pills, the knife have both come from the sand, and other than the flashlight, he hasn't thought about what he's put into it already, what he could put into it next. A memory comes to him again, a vague sense of putting a full beer can into the sand, watching it sink, but he can't be sure if that's real or a dream.

He thinks about when he found the pills.

"I guess, maybe I bled into it? That one was a total accident, we were trying to dig in it—"

"Don't." Nick turns suddenly, some of his beer sloshing from the neck to crawl in rivulets down his hand. "Sorry, but don't do that. Don't dig in it, with your hands, I mean. Don't put your body into it."

Trevor's shoulder grows warm, and the lesion pulses, and he knows he will ignore this advice, might ignore all of Nick's advice. Even as he's having this thought, he shakes his head, and it dissipates, evaporates into wispy tendrils of mental smoke.

"Anyway, the day after I bled into it, I found a bottle of Vicodin in the yard. Walter's name was on it."

Nick upturns his beer and drains the mostly full bottle, his neck pulsing hard with each swallow.

"I think," he says, drops the bottle to the grass, "it's time we switch to bourbon, Trevor."

16.

FRAN SWEEPS MELISSA into the house like an updraft, the woman's energy pulling everything around her into her wake. The house is just full enough to make swift movement uncomfortable, a bustling menagerie of people drinking, lounging on the couch, working in the kitchen.

"I'll give you the fifty-cent tour," Fran says, her teeth pink with rosé, her eyes gleaming like a child at show and tell. The house is stuffed with not just plants but *things,* an organized cacophony that seems ready to topple at any moment. Bookshelves hemorrhage old leather volumes and dogeared paperbacks with equal abandon, any rhyme or reason to their organization tossed to the wind. *Trevor would have a conniption fit,* Melissa thinks and smiles about it, about him, about the paradox of his own accumulation of *things* mixed with his innate need to keep them organized. She drinks from her wine glass, the wine light and sweet and already going to her head. She needs to eat, assumes they'll end the tour in the kitchen, so carefully weighs each step while her head spins trying to take in everything in the small, crowded house.

Indoor plants fill the gaps in possessions, hanging in baskets from the ceiling, stuffed into plant stands, in free standing pots. One corner seems pulled out of a magazine of the southwest, terra cotta pots boasting big, reaching cacti, and the dirt stuffed with porcelain figures of men in comically stereotypical sombreros and ponchos.

Melissa follows Fran through this, what must be the living room or some approximation of it, and thinks of how it truly is a living room, is truly for living, and resolves to ask Fran for tips on plants, maybe even ask her to go with her to a nursery to pick out some that would thrive in the low amount of natural light that comes through the window into their own living room.

Melissa follows Fran to weave upstairs into a hallway where the older woman only allows Melissa glimpses of a bathroom, bedrooms, all with some variation and arrangement of plants, though it's clear that the bulk of the indoor plants live downstairs on the first floor.

"You live here alone, Fran?" Melissa asks, realizing her insensitivity too late. If it's rude, Fran either doesn't seem to notice or is accustomed to this type of question.

"I do, yeah. I've had roommates float in and out throughout the years, but I'm the one constant, I guess. I won't change for anybody," she says, leading Melissa back down the stairs, "so to live here with me, you have to be a certain kind of person."

"I think this is *incredible*," Melissa says, and she means it, isn't just allowing the wine to speak for her. On the short tour, she's decided that their house, despite being new and exciting, needs something else in it, needs something else living in it, something like this, something alive. More than that, she thinks she needs a hobby, something to distract her, consume her, keep her away from the hole.

The hole. She realizes that she has been properly distracted, lost in this world of life inside of Fran's house, but her hand taps a spot on her leg, a spot where she can feel the new bruise growing, pulsing.

She drains her glass in one gulp.

"That's the spirit," Fran says. She puts an arm around Melissa's shoulder and leads her into the kitchen. The people have largely cleared out, the last of them shuffle through the screen door holding a tray of something golden-brown and steaming as they enter from the living room. Fran opens the fridge, pulls out a half-empty bottle, refills both their glasses higher than polite company would generally allow.

"This is an annual thing, this party?"

Fran takes a sip, tops off her glass, puts the bottle back in the fridge. She nods. "Oh yeah, at least one a year. If weather and health allows, I try to have one at the beginning of the summer, then this one at the end. You know, kind of bookend the summer, if that makes sense."

It makes a sort of sense to Melissa, even if it doesn't make the same kind of sense, so she nods.

"I started it when I moved here. It really was a way for me to try to meet all the neighbors," Fran continues, "and now it's that if someone new moves in," she reaches her glass across the space between them to clink Melissa's, "but if I'm being honest, it's largely an excuse to show off my yard and my house, show off my plants."

Melissa wants to detect something lonely, almost desperate in this, but can't find it in Fran's tone or her eyes. She thinks about living alone, thinks about Brody and Trevor gone, shivers and bristles with excitement in equal measure. Her heart swells with horror and shame, as it never occurred to her to think of her life as any different than exactly how it is, never thought of steering it at all. It's as if her hands have been at her sides rather than on the wheel, a thought that sends her to the wine glass again.

"Feel free to eat whatever you want," Fran says, and Melissa notices for the first time that there are still trays covering the countertops, each piled with an assortment of meats, cheeses, vegetables. Both of them pick something up from a tray and pop it in their mouths, stand alone chewing in the kitchen, the music throbbing outside, the party guests milling around in the afternoon sun.

"So," Fran finally says, and Melissa thinks that she knows what she's going to ask, is prepared somehow for everyone at the party to have noticed her bruise despite it being under her jeans, noticed Trevor's seeping wound. "How do you like Walt's house?"

Strangest, she notices, is the neighborhood's insistence on calling it *Walt's House*—capitalized, proper noun, formal—despite him being gone, gone insane, insanely gone.

"Oh, we love it. Everyone here has been so nice, case in point," she is the one to bridge the distance this time, the clink of the wine glasses filling the silence. "There are a handful of projects, little things he let go, but the house is beautiful. I think our first big project is putting up a fence in the backyard between us and the restaurant. Trevor thinks he saw someone wandering the yard a few nights ago, like a drunk got lost and walked through the yard."

She pauses like to stall, hoping Fran doesn't hear the missing parts of her description, the big project they can't seem to figure out, might not want to tackle, might love and cherish and worship and feed.

Feed?

She blinks—too fast she thinks, Fran will be able to tell something's wrong—and shakes her head to clear it. She takes half her wine in such a hurry that she chokes, small dribbles escaping her lips to fall to the linoleum.

Fran doesn't notice, never breaks eye contact.

"Did the realtor tell you what happened to Walt? Why he couldn't live there anymore?"

Realtors, Melissa thinks, don't have to disclose mental illness, do they? Just death on the property, accidents, suicides, murders, dismemberments.

Bottomless pits?

"Tammy didn't say anything specific, no. Just that he was selling because it was too much for him. The Grubers said he went nuts, dementia, I think."

Fran snorts, chokes on her own wine. "Sorry, they're nosy little shits. Of course they would rush to gossip with you."

Melissa swirls the dregs of her wine, stares into it.

"I feel like you asked because you know something and want to tell me."

Fran's eyes grow serious, almost cold. Melissa tries to resist another filling of the wine glass, but Fran muscles the neck past her protesting hand and slops the glass half full.

"He definitely had something, they're not lying about that. I don't know if it was dementia, though."

"You knew him, then?"

"Yeah, I knew him. We all knew him." She waves her hand in the air like to indicate the block. "Nice guy. Quiet. Mostly kept to himself, so I guess if something was going on and we didn't notice, we can be somewhat excused. Though we should take care of our own, you know?"

"You've been very welcoming, but everyone we meet keeps calling it Walt's House, like it'll never belong to us. I know we haven't been here very long, but still."

"Ah, shit, I did that too, didn't I? I'm sorry. He lived here for so long, it's a force of habit, I guess. No one holds anything against you for it, I'm sure of it. Just hard to break that habit. He was here when I got here, so it's weird to not have him down there at the end of the block, is all. People will get used to it, and we're all glad he's getting the help he needs, or at least we hope he is."

"What happened to him?"

"Well," Fran drains her glass again, the rosé having reached her eyes to rim them in red, "he was going through something, but no one knows if there was an inciting incident or anything. As far as I know there wasn't. His wife left him before I ever met him, and from all I could tell, he liked living alone, liked being part of the block and all. Nick told me that things started going wrong with the house, projects, like you call them."

Melissa says nothing, waits for the bomb to drop, waits for Fran to say that Walt was covered in strange sores, ran naked through the streets screaming, told them all about some unfillable bottomless pit in the backyard of the house.

"He had to replace the well pump is what I heard, and after digging that out himself in the backyard, his back started bothering him. The doctor gave him pain pills that were too strong, got himself addicted to them, you know how it goes. If weed was legal . . . "

She trails off, stalling.

"So is that what everyone called dementia, opioid addiction?" Melissa doesn't know if this makes her feel better or worse. Was Walt taking the pills for his back, or to cloud the idea of something else?

"Well, yeah, I guess you could say that. Folks like the Grubers probably thought he was going nuts, don't have the sympathy to care for an addict, you know. It doesn't compute with them that he's still a person under that fog. The final straw, though, I think people could attribute to those pills, and I'm sure I don't have to tell you that it was the Grubers who called the police."

Melissa shudders, hugs herself to stave off the sudden cold she feels.

"The police?"

Fran nods. "One night they hear screaming, constant, loud screaming like Walt is being murdered, but by the time the police get there he's just sobbing, can't make any sentences worth listening to, so they called his son, and he threw him in a home."

"Why was he screaming?"

Fran shrugs. "None of us know. Like I said, he wasn't making sense, wasn't making full sentences at that point, just crying in the backyard."

"They found him in the backyard?"

"When the police got there, he had dug up the yard, dug into the sand mound for the septic, and was half buried, crying and screaming. The way I hear it, he was up to his chest in the sand somehow."

Melissa goes cold, thinks of the pit, thinks of sinking into it, surrendering to it, feeding it, and claps a hand to her leg, to the bruise there growing warm and moist.

Fran shakes her head, remembering. "And the weird thing—weirder than it already was, I mean—is that he dug down there with no shoes on, completely barefoot, and somehow shredded his pants legs in the process. His legs were all torn up, bloody and cut from knee to toe."

Melissa wants to ask a thousand questions, wants to know where Walt is now, if he talked, what he said happened, but before she can, the screen door whap-clacks open and shut, and Frank Gruber rushes into the kitchen, his face pale and Tommy at his side. The kid's right hand is held above his head and masked in blood.

"Holy shit, Frank! What happened?" Fran sets down her wine glass and runs the tap, grabbing a rag and pushing it to Tommy's hand.

"He was running and fell against some of the chicken wire. I think he'll be fine, but it's torn up pretty good."

"Okay, don't worry, I've got alcohol and antiseptic and band aids," Fran rattles off more medical supplies, running down the laundry list, rushes Frank and Tommy into the bathroom in the hall.

Melissa stands in shock, wine glass still clutched in her hand, but not in shock over Tommy, the blood. Front and center in her mind is a picture of an old man chest deep in the sand behind his house, her house, screaming as his legs are torn up from below.

She looks out the door, looks for Trevor, for Brody, looks for any familiar face that can buoy her in this mental storm, and catches her husband's back as he leaves the yard. With him is an older man she hasn't met yet, close cropped hair and a clean flannel shirt, who looks back at the house for a beat, a brief moment of eye contact, before ushering her husband out of the party and down the block.

17.

IF FRAN'S HOUSE is a monument to excess, Nick's is an exercise in restraint. They enter through the side door, cutting into the yard between Nick's and the Wyngard house. So much about all the houses on the block is similar to their house, Trevor notes, as they enter a kitchen that seems to spill into a dining room.

Unlike their house, everything in Nick's seems to be a shrine to the nineteen seventies. Where the kitchen meets the dining room, the tile floor surrenders to thick shag carpet, all the colors he can see from the next room melding together in comforting shades of brown, orange, yellow. A brown couch boasts drawings of cowboys, horses, Indians. The cabinets are rough wood, the finish a natural patina worn down with age and care rather than intention. The formica countertops are a burnt orange, the stove an old gas range.

Nick opens a cabinet and pulls down two glasses, each with a different animal painted on the front, a description of said animal on the back. Nick fills each with a few fingers of bourbon from a bottle he materializes, and Trevor turns the glass in his hand, admiring the design.

Nick notices and gestures to the closed cabinet. "Found a whole set at a yard sale, I've got six of them."

Nick's glass, Trevor sees, is decorated with an American bison, his own a coyote.

They sit at the table, a worn and pock-marked slab of hardwood, and Nick brings the bottle. Trevor sips the liquor, and it's like his body is full of Christmas lights that all turn on at once, a warm glow emanating from inside.

For a while, that's all it is, the two men sharing a drink in a dated kitchen, the only noise the slow crunch of gravel from an occasional car crawling down Hollenbach Road. When their glasses are empty, Nick fills them again, a little higher this time, the wet pop of the cork like a slammed door in the quiet kitchen.

"I was the one who found Walt the night they took him away," Nick says, and it's like the silence was a prelude, the foreplay before the main event.

Trevor opens his mouth to speak, to release the torrent of thoughts and unanswered questions held there, but Nick holds a hand up, less halting and more gentle.

"I know you have questions, and I'm sure you already think you know everything, but I was here for it, at least the once, so before you think you know what's going on back there you should hear it. That fair?"

Trevor thinks that's more than fair, and he nods to indicate as much, cradles his glass in two hands on the table like to keep it safe, like it might fly away, disappear, burst into shards. He doesn't know much about whiskey but can tell this is good stuff by the way it goes down smooth and is already rounding off the sharp edges of the world. He takes a chance, gets comfortable, and reaches for the bottle himself, holding it out to Nick first in deference. Nick knocks back his glass, the amber liquid disappearing under the thick of his mustache, then holds out his glass and nods. Trevor fills them both, and they lean back, the chairs groaning in harmony beneath their weight.

"Walt didn't come to me about it, not at first, but we were friends, you know? Not close, nothing like that, but real friends, not like Frank Gruber thinks they were friends." He smiles and Trevor returns it, but neither laughs. "He'd been in Vietnam, but you wouldn't know it to look at him or talk to him. He wasn't big on talking about it, for obvious reasons." He waves his glass in the air as if this gesture could capture the enormity of war, the weight of the repercussions. "I wasn't in the service, but I guess I come off that way. Spent my time in a bike club, but I got out clean and luckily with nothing too terrible on my conscience to keep me up nights. I guess all this is to say that I seemed like the most trustworthy one, the one he could come to when he found the hole."

Just like that, there it is: an outright acknowledgement of the hole. The words are spoken in the real world, and Trevor doesn't know if he feels like crying or screaming or leaving, so he settles for another sip of whiskey and waves for Nick to continue.

"I'm assuming you haven't gone to anyone yet, judging by how you reacted when I mentioned it back at Fran's, and Walt didn't come to me immediately either. It's a weird thing," Nick says, and he lets these words hang while he swirls the whiskey in his glass, and Trevor doesn't know if he's referring to the hole as weird—categorizing it as the geographical anomaly that it is—or the situation as weird— the way different men interpret it, deal with it, feed it, the way different men fill the hole—so he asks as much.

Nick chuckles dryly. "Well, both, I guess. Both are weird. But you already know the hole is weird. I was going to say that it's a weird thing the way the thing seems to not *want* you to go to anyone about it. Do you feel that? I know Walt did."

Trevor knows exactly what he means, feels it deep, bone-deep, and, in acknowledging it, feels a pull toward home as if a fishing line is attached to his heart and his brain and has just been tugged, guiding him back.

Nick notices the far-off look in Trevor's eyes, the way his body stiffens, and nods. "Yeah, I suppose you do feel that. Walt found it hard to explain, hard to quantify, the way the thing called out to him. We called it a lot of things when we talked about it, the hole, the sand pit, the Sarlacc, but he always fell back on calling it his void. Not *the* void, but specifically *his* void, and he described it to me like that once, like an emptiness inside him had been drawn into the world, made manifest, escaped him and taken root in the yard."

"Was it there when he moved in?" Trevor asks.

Nick shakes his head, not like saying no, but like trying to dislodge some memory stuck like popcorn in a back tooth.

"He claimed it wasn't, but I tend to think it was, and maybe he didn't notice it, or it didn't work its way up right away, laid dormant, almost, if that makes any kind of sense."

Trevor nods, knows it makes all the sense in the world.

"If you want to know what I really think," Nick says, leaning forward, meaty, tattooed arms resting on the table, "I think that it's maybe *always* been there, like deep down in there, and only chooses to show itself when it wants to."

Trevor leans on the table to meet his eyes, their faces only a foot apart, the space between filled with musk and whiskey breath.

"You mean you think it's *sentient*?"

Nick leans back, breaks the tension, swigs. "Who knows, man, I don't live there, I don't feel the pull the way you do, the way Walt did, but I believe you, you know? And if it's like he said, then you're also getting messages sent to you, beamed to you, whatever the fuck, almost like telepathy. Is that close to what it's like?"

Trevor thinks of the urges he's had lately, the impulses, subtle changes in his demeanor that Melissa has picked up on that he might not have noticed otherwise.

Melissa.

She's changing too, isn't she? He noticed just that morning her hand going to her leg almost subconsciously, and he would bet money that there's a bruise growing there, a weeping sore waiting to open and taste the air.

Almost like he can read his mind, Nick tips his glass toward Trevor's shoulder.

"Is that one of the wounds?"

Trevor looks down, and his grey t-shirt is darkened and moving, rising and falling like that elementary school pig lung, like the pit. He slaps a hand to it like to hide it, like to lock the barn door after the horse is four counties away.

"Sorry, sorry. Don't get weird about this stuff now," Nick says, his hands raised up in defense. "Walt had one, at first, then I know he had a bunch more, near the end."

Another silence, thick as molasses, then Trevor pulls his shirt up and over his head and Nick gasps.

The original sore, the first one, is the most active, breathing from his shoulder and weeping a thick yellow pus, translucent rivulets running down his arm like tears, the liquid dotted with grains of sand. Peppered across his torso are another dozen at least, the number lost to Trevor a few days ago, all in different stages of bruising, swelling, birthing.

Nick pulls a pair of glasses from his flannel pocket and perches them on his nose, leans forward to get a better look.

"Holy shit, man. Walt told me about his, showed me the first one, but I never saw the others on him. Only knew they were there because he told me, and when I found him they were bleeding, *seeping* through his shirt. I've never seen anything like this."

He reaches slowly like to touch the hole on Trevor's shoulder, the breathing one, his eyes glazing over behind his lenses. Trevor grabs his finger, not rough but firm, and Nick is shocked out of it, brought back to life, to the kitchen.

"I wouldn't do that," Trevor says, and beamed into his brain is an image of Melissa putting her finger in it, feeling it suckle, swallow. It makes him think of the bruises he's sure now grow on Melissa, the plague they both bear. Simultaneous but almost unconscious is the thought that Nick isn't worthy, that he doesn't *deserve* to touch the hole, hasn't sat by the altar and worshiped like he has, hasn't given to it. Fed it.

Nick shakes his head like coming out of a deep sleep.

"Yeah, I guess you're right. We don't know everything about this thing yet, I guess. Damn. Went somewhere else for a second. If you'll excuse me."

He pushes back his chair and runs the tap, the house coming alive with the sound of groaning pipes and rushing water. He washes his face and presses a towel to it, standing blind by the sink for a few seconds before sitting back down and refilling their glasses. Trevor's shirt is back on, and the moment, whatever it was, has passed for now, and they return to the relative weirdness of only discussing the hole in abstract, not seeing, touching, feeling it.

"Okay, I'm back. Let's tackle this thing with logic, what do you say?"

Trevor thinks that sounds fucking absurd when he is becoming a living manifestation, an acolyte, of a sentient, bottomless pit in his backyard, but he nods.

"You said the first thing you put into it was blood?"

"It wasn't intentional, but yeah, when we first found it we tried to dig and get rid of it, we thought it was a dumped sandbox, something left over from the previous owner, from Walt."

I'm sorry, we didn't know, he thinks, sends into the air, and he thinks he can feel the mouth on his shoulder grow warm in understanding.

Nick cups a hand on his chin, strokes his short beard. "I wonder if that's the connection, the reason for the sores. It has part of you, something from your body inside it now." He shakes his head, chuckles a little. "I could also be making connections that aren't there, looking for a logic in something that's so completely unexplainable that it doesn't fucking matter at all, but it feels like there has to be some kind of internal logic to it, doesn't there?"

Trevor shrugs, and they drink, but he thinks, somewhere inside where the real Trevor still operates independent of the hole, that Nick might be onto something. He's not sure what Melissa would have given to the hole, if she bled or pissed or spit into it.

The memory hits him like a truck, a full scene presented in a full color flash that only takes a second, Melissa putting her finger in the open sore of his shoulder, them shirking their clothes and fucking in the sand on top of the hole, and he wants to weep.

"What did it give you for the blood?" Nick asks.

"What?" Trevor looks up and is confused for a moment, then thinks to what Nick said in Fran's yard, the cost of the knife, and can't believe he hasn't put these pieces together on his own—that the pit is a barter system, some eldritch trading post where goods are exchanged. He stammers, the words heavy like glue in his mouth. "Vicodin."

Nick leans back and nods. "Vicodin is a weird response to blood, I guess. That's not normally how you treat a cut, but there I go thinking that this thing exists in some sort of logical space again."

"A few days before, I twisted my ankle, I stepped in the sand while mowing the lawn, that's how we found it in the first place. It wasn't out in the open at that point, I would bet money on it. It was under grass until I stepped in it."

"I'm guessing the Vicodin was Walt's?"

Trevor shrugs, nods. "His name was on it, at least." A thought hits him. "What did he get for the Vicodin?"

Nick shakes his head, swirls his glass. "Honestly, by the time he was getting things from it, had figured out the quid pro quo as it were, he wasn't telling me as much about it. He talked to me a lot when he first found it, and we tried a lot of shit to get rid of it."

Trevor perks up. "All we tried to do so far was shovel it into buckets and throw it down the bank. Did anything you do work?"

Nick laughs. "It's still there, so what do you think? He built a small foundation out of cinder blocks at first, mortared it and everything, and after a day or two it crumbled and disappeared, sucked into it." He shakes his head, living in the memories. "I can't even tell you how

70

many bags of Quikrete we mixed up and threw down there, trying to jam up the works, fill it up, whatever. We didn't know anything about what it was at that point. It was just a weird sand hole, just, what's the word, an anomaly."

Trevor sighs, sits back, defeat showing on his face.

"So I'm not sure what he got back for them," Nick says, "but I know he at least put his pills and that knife in." He drains his glass, considers the bottle, decides against it. "Until himself."

Trevor sits forward with a jolt. "What?"

"That's how I found him," Nick says, changing his mind and emptying the rest of the bottle into their glasses. The room reeks of whiskey and the low fug of sweat, the scent filling the air between them. "Frank Gruber will tell you that he heard the screaming, that he called the police, but I was the first to actually go over there."

He looks up, the edges of his eyes glistening with water.

"He was waist-deep in the sand, screaming and crying, those sores soaking through his t-shirt."

Trevor says nothing, so after a moment, Nick continues.

"It seems, if I had to guess, that he didn't have anything else to give." He raises the glass like to drink, stops with it blocking his mouth and speaks in a voice so low it's almost a whisper. "He gave it everything, and it still wouldn't take him."

18.

MELISSA COLLECTS BRODY, a sweaty mess of grass stains and scratches, from the backyard soon after the Grubers come barreling into the kitchen. When Tommy appears, his hand gloved in blood, it's a few moments before she thinks of her own child, the potential danger, and she is embarrassed by how long it takes her to stumble outside, the wine still stomping riot through her blood, and find him crouched behind one of the garden boxes at the back of the yard.

"Hide, Mommy!" he shrieks, and at first she starts to duck, starts to look around with her head on a swivel before realizing he's still fully immersed in the game, that hide and seek is his prime operative.

"I think we're going to get ready to go, honey," she says. She scoops him despite his protests and staggers under the weight at first, regaining her balance to carry him back through the yard. She wants to find Fran, thank her for a lovely party, but remembers that she's in her bathroom, the makeshift rural triage, and decides to stage an Irish goodbye, come back around in a few days with cookies to thank her for her kindness.

Melissa gathers their things, struggling to bag their canvas chairs with Brody tugging at her hand and trying to rejoin the fray at the back of the yard. The cooler is still weighty, and she reflects that Trevor must not have had time to drink many beers before that stranger with the greying hair whisked him away to who-knows-where, left her to handle Brody, the chairs, the everything of it all. She considers wheeling the cooler straight into the backyard and dropping each sweating can, one by one, into the pit, watching the otherworldly thing swallow them each in turn, the sand clumping and gathering on the wet aluminum, and this makes her laugh, a low chuckle that rolls into a bark and by the time she realizes that she's laughing with the full force of her belly, she is out the gate, down the walk, and back into the street.

Brody in one hand, the chairs slung across her back, the cooler trailing behind and crunching in the gravel, she finds herself wondering which house the grey-haired stranger lives in, what they're talking about, where her husband is, and then the door to a blue house set back off the road opens and the two of them are standing in the doorway, both wearing grave expressions and wobbling on their feet.

"Daddy!" Brody yells, breaking free from her grip. The shift in balance is such that she almost topples over, spills herself into the street, and the thought of her lying in the middle of the lane surrounded by ice and beer cans makes her bark a laugh again, a laugh that draws the attention of both men, so she trundles the cooler and chairs off the road and into the stranger's yard.

Trevor is drunk, that much she can see, but her own wine-based barks of laughter keep her from judging. She watches his wobble when he crouches to intercept Brody and takes a few seconds to get to his feet when he stands holding him.

"Nick, this is my wife, Melissa," Trevor says, and Melissa walks slowly up the two steps to the porch, shakes his hand with both of hers now that they're liberated from Brody and the cooler.

"It's nice to put another face on one of these houses," she says, and Trevor smiles at her, eyes narrowed. She didn't say the phrase weirdly on purpose but now is glad she did, is happy to have broken Trevor and Nick from whatever moody cloud they were in when she arrived.

73

"The pleasure is all mine, Mrs. Davis," Nick says, polite as a school child, and she likes him immediately, but that doesn't stop her uninhibited mind and tongue from launching questions blunt as a hammer.

"What have you been doing with my husband, Mr . . . "

"Harper," Nick fills in, and she sees his eyes shift from her to her husband almost like for permission, sees a subtle nod pass between them. "Sorry to have stolen your husband from the party. I hope we didn't inconvenience you by leaving you alone with young master Brody here." He reaches out and musses Brody's hair, the child laughing and chanting 'master!'

She laughs. She can't help it. Even in the face of the absurdity of the party, of Fran, the bloody Gruber, her whole goddamn life since moving to Hollenbach Road, she laughs.

"You act like I'm not used to it," she says, realizing too late that the jab could come off biting. Out of the corner of her eye, she keeps vigilant for a wince from Trevor, is relieved when she doesn't see one. "He's a handful, but he's our handful. Do you have children, Mr. Harper?"

His smile is wry, but Melissa detects no trace of regret. "No ma'am, don't think I was ever quite built for them." He ruffles Brody's hair again. "I was just sending your husband off with a nightcap, and we were discussing Walter Henderson, the man you bought your house from. He was a friend of mine."

She stiffens, hopes it doesn't show. "Oh, I was sorry to hear what happened to him. I hope he's getting the care he needs."

Both men raise eyebrows, their collective questions living on their faces, but neither asks them. When the silence breaks, it's Nick who does it.

"Yes, me too. From what I understand, he's quite comfortable."

His words drift over them like a fog, cloaking all of their minds until Brody starts to squirm and squeal.

"We better get him home, Trevor," Melissa says. She steps backwards off the porch, down to reclaim the cooler. "It was nice to meet you, Mr. Harper. Hopefully we'll get to see you again soon."

"Come over for a beer sometime," Trevor says, Brody fighting to get out of his arms. He relents and lets him run to Melissa who clenches his hand tight, the road only a few steps away.

"I'll take you up on that," Nick says. "Careful getting home." He steps back into the house and closes the door, and the early evening goes quiet again.

19

THOUGH HIS ANKLE is healed, Trevor keeps Walter Henderson's expired Vicodin on him near constantly, a pill here and there helping him blur the edges of his perception, helping him push the hole from his mind when the temptation to experiment becomes overwhelming. He wants to take everything they own out to the yard, systematically feed items to the hole and catalog them, keep a journal of the exchange rate. Part of him, even in lieu of everything, is doubtful of the rules—the supernatural providence of the pit—and dismisses this nagging desire as absurd. When he notices these urges, he takes a pill. They buoy his work, also, he tells himself, amping up his internal drummer and allowing him to type at a frantic rhythm.

The pills have doubled in quantity in the clear orange vial, not from supernatural means but because he took them all out and cut each into quarters with the bone handle knife, explaining to himself that they aren't a problem at that size—he doesn't have a problem, he's not the problem, there's no problem.

A clack brings him back, the clack of blocks, the tell-tale sound of his son's brain-dead playing on the rug beneath him. A rare day, one he has come to despise, one where Brody's daycare is closed, but Melissa works, and he is left as the sole charge for the tiny human for a whole day, his balance of work-drink-work-contemplate-the-hole interrupted by parental duty.

He looks down into the child's eyes and thinks that maybe, just maybe he can see what strangers do, what doting family members do, when they say things like "he's got your eyes, he's got your nose, he looks just like you."

Trevor thinks, not for the first time, of the selfishness inherent in needing one that looks just like you, one full to bursting with your blood, your family's blood, your arrogant entitled blood. His blood is shit, a lazy river of alcohol dotted with blood cell rafts along for the ride.

Adoption is less selfish, but he was never really open to that either, just held it as a convenient opinion, an altruistic stance to take because he knows how hard, how frustrating, how expensive the process is and assumes he would never be called to the mat on it.

Raising a monster you made is one thing. He can't imagine paying for one only for it to turn out like him.

Looking at his watch, he decides he needs a drink.

One sweating beer is cracked immediately, and another goes into the holster of his back pocket, then he thinks for a second and grabs a third, preferring a room temperature swig to getting up again in a handful of minutes. To that end, he heads to the bathroom to empty his bladder in anticipation of new liquid.

So strong is his stream that he almost doesn't register the screen door at all, almost passes it off as a house settling noise, a neighborhood noise, a truck-hitting-a-pothole-in-the-street-out-front noise, then remembers where they're living, the idyllic country home he pushed so hard for, and cocks his head like waiting for the noise to repeat. When it doesn't, he shrugs it off as an anomaly, so used to Melissa being here, the door opening and closing a thousand times a day as his family splits their time between the house and yard.

His family.

He remembers, registers that Brody is home alone with him, just in time to catch the little shit running—wobbling,

77

really, the best he can on his under-formed toddler legs—through the yard, something clutched in his pudgy hand.

The pill bottle.

It would be just his luck for Melissa to come home right now, for some well-meaning neighbor to see their two-year-old son running through the backyard shaking a bottle of Vicodin like some pharmaceutical maraca. He shakes off—laughs at the synchronicity, the symmetry of the shaking—and zips up, finishing his beer while pushing through the screen door.

Brody is halfway through the yard by the time Trevor's feet hit the grass and he knows, even if Brody doesn't know, that the pill bottle is headed for the sand pit. He doesn't know if the sand has the same pull over Brody, hasn't even considered it, but now he is filled with dread at the thought that the pit might actually be malicious the way Nick implied and that Brody might be its terrestrial agent sent to work against him. If the sand can influence him to feed things to it, to break out in sores and welts and push his mind to think of violence, then it stands that it could creep into Brody's mind, turn him against him, send him to steal back the pills and return them to whence they came.

Almost as if they know they're being considered, can hear his thoughts, the sores on his body open and weep, the pus slicking his skin and soaking into his shirt.

Maybe he wasn't grateful enough for the pills, the healing offering that the pit gave to him in return for twisting his ankle, shedding his blood. He'd only fed it the flashlight and the beer after all. The flashlight had been a mistake, an accidental offering before he knew what the pit was, knew the rules, and he still isn't sure about the beer, can't validate the memory that hangs lazily in his head like a fog.

Bullshit, he thinks, shaking his head and pulling his mind back to the present. The pit loves him, chose his yard to manifest in, calls to him, marked him, *chose* him—show of gratitude or not—and there was no way he was going to let some little shit that sprung from his loins disrespect the god in his garden by returning a gift in such a crude and thoughtless way.

"Brody! C'mon buddy, let's go back in the house!"

Brody doesn't respond to the sound of his voice, the call sounding somewhere between a caring parent and coaxing a sow to the abattoir. Half-formed words fly from his mouth in unintelligible toddler babble, the kid laughing, actually *laughing*, running full tilt to discard the bottle.

Trevor doesn't run, conscious even in his rattled state that diners at the All-Weather, the Grubers, anybody could see him until he crosses into the back half of the yard, and even there he isn't completely shrouded, is partially exposed. When he's hidden by the boughs of the large overhanging pines, he quickens his pace trying to close the distance between them before Brody gets to the pit.

Even over the pounding in his head, he can hear the pills shake in the bottle in the kid's tiny hand, the rhythm matching his footfalls, matching the beat of his heart, the pulse of the sores, the rhythm of the world.

Brody is a foot away from the sand, his hand reeling back like a major league pitcher in the ninth, and in a last push of desperation and abandon, Trevor launches headfirst, leaving his feet and tackling Brody to the grass.

Something crunches under him, doesn't crack or break but crunches, and Brody starts to whimper, the first notes of a good cry revving up harsh and soulful in his tiny chest. Trevor watches the sun catch the bottle and refract through the translucent plastic, the light catching all the scratches, dings, and wear in the bottle as it arcs, falls, bounces, lands on the end of the pit in the beginning of the sand. Brody still under him, Trevor reaches, stretches, his fingers grazing the bottle and rolling it, and he thinks that if he can get the pad of his finger on the lid, the white ridges that rim the cap, he can roll it toward him and get it off the sand, but the grains start to move and run, carrying the pill bottle closer to the center of the pit and out of reach.

"No no no no, goddamn it, Brody, you little shit!"

Trevor rises onto his hands and knees and crawls to the pit, but the bottle is already starting to sink back down into the sand. He digs, frantic, like a dog tearing lawn, and he supposes that is exactly what he is, sand flying out from his hands and between his legs.

Like before, the sand shows no progress. No matter how much of it is cast aside under the manic digging of his hands, the pit remains the same, and the bottle is fully submerged now, gone from his sight. In a fit of desperation, he plunges his arm into the pit, the sand giving way easily as if to receive him, and sinks up to the shoulder, his chest flat against the grass. He paws through the sand, warm and moist this far down, a mountain man noodling for catfish, and his fingers graze something hard and cool and he maneuvers his fingers to grip the bottle, a smile breaking across his sweaty face.

"I got it! Shit, fuck, Brody, don't cry. I got it, it'll all be okay," he says, his words escaping in breathy streams and running together like the pleas of a madman, and he starts laughing until he tries to pull his hand from the hole.

There's no pressure, nothing physically holding his hand, but he is unable to budge from his position on the ground, his arm fully submerged, taken, consumed by the hole. Panic is slow to set in, the emotion detoured by the beer chugged in the bathroom, but when it sets in, it sets in hard, and he flails his other limbs, pulling desperately on the buried arm.

"Brody, help. Hey, buddy, here, look at me."

Brody cries on the grass, his wails now a whimper, big bubbles of snot expanding to pop on his upper lip, his whole face wet and glistening with pain and fear. He looks up at Trevor, but Trevor thinks he's somewhere else—not here in the grass with his trapped father.

"Brody, I need you to go to the shed, get a shovel, help me loosen some of the sand that's holding Daddy in, okay?"

Brody just stares, his crying quieting now, his pained expression turning into what Trevor swears is a satisfied grin—an evil leer—the face of someone possessed who knows exactly what they're doing and has him exactly where they want him.

"Fuck, Brody. No, c'mon, help Daddy. Can you do that?" In his desperation, he resorts to a compromise on his banned baby-talk edict, letting syrup slip into his voice in an attempt to sway the boy back to his side, to pull him from being an agent of the pit. Brody stands with real effort, testing shaky legs like a drunk coming back to life for a second round in the ring.

"Yes, that's it, buddy—the shed, the shovel. C'mon, help Daddy." Trevor is breathing hard now, his shoulder aching from the strain of pulling against an invisible enemy, his hand still clenched on the pill bottle deep in the dark earth. He thinks of a movie he saw, a man stuck with his arm in a rock in the desert somewhere, and wonders if he could reach the knife, if things were dire enough to cut off his own arm, if he possessed the constitution, the strength, to saw through his shoulder with a hunting knife.

Instead of heading toward the shed, Brody waddles closer to Trevor, almost within reach, and slowly begins to circle him, his eyes never leaving those of his father.

"What are you doing? Go to the shed, buddy. C'mon, you have to get Daddy out of here." Sweat is pouring down his face now, the sand darkening under him from moisture, each droplet that hits the surface sucked into the hole. Brody continues his circle, his pace growing more confident, steadier.

"Stay back—keep away from me, you little shit," Trevor says, the honey gone from his voice now, his panicked brain convinced that the hole has fully consumed Brody, that this creature, this *thing*, is not his son. It might be the first time—certainly the strongest time—that he can identify and feel a connection with Brody, the real Brody, as his child, his offspring. Seeing this version—this perversion—of his child, his anger and fear are tempered with a deep well of sadness, a late-stage disappointment that here, at the end, he never knew his son before he was fully consumed.

Brody's circle tightens, getting closer to Trevor, and Trevor rotates his body in the sand keeping his legs out of reach of the foul child, a plan forming in his mind. His face is turned toward the Grubers' fence, his legs splayed like dowsing rods pointing toward the river, and when Brody's circling brings him between Trevor and the bank, Trevor pulls his knee up toward his chest and kicks out like a horse, connecting with Brody's chest, his full strength pulsing through his leg.

Brody's tiny body is nearly lifted off the ground, his toes reaching to maintain some kind of earthly contact. He flies backwards, staggering like only a two-year-old can, and for a second, he is weightless—a vampire hovering outside a second story window, an apparition come to call, floating in the air between the earth and sky—then he's falling, tumbling, rolling down the bank and out of sight.

Trevor cheers, this victory against the pit clouding what he's done, distorting the act in his mind to become self-defense, his only child kicked clean off of this plane of existence. He pulls again and thinks he feels his arm budge, thinks he can feel the grip of the pit begin to loosen, then something sharp and hot closes around the knuckles of his index and middle fingers. He has just enough time to remember Walter Henderson screaming, half submerged, before the thing closes, clamps, bites down, and takes off his first two fingers.

The remnants of his hand let go of the pill bottle, the plastic slick with blood, and he pulls up and out, the pit releasing his arm at last. Blood pumps from his fingers in grisly pulses and he shoves his remaining fist, his whole unmangled fist, into his mouth to stifle the scream, to not draw attention to this absurd scene, this tableau of domestic violence and dehumanization, to not draw attention to the fact that he just kicked his two-year-old son off the edge of the world—maybe into the river, maybe to drown, sink, float all the way to Philadelphia like they irrationally feared.

Trevor peels his flannel shirt off and wraps it around his maimed hand, the blood instantly soaking the worn fabric. He sits down hard, unsure what to do next, when he hears Brody begin to cry out from the bottom of the bank.

20

MELISSA PARKS THE CAR and pulls the groceries from the trunk, balancing the bags in the crook of an arm and reaching out for the doorknob with the other, finds it locked.

"Goddammit, Trevor," she mumbles, but it's through a smile, since she's the one who asked him to lock the door when he was home alone with Brody, isn't she, and maybe he's finally taking initiative with the kid.

Many of their friends—the ones they had in the suburbs before the move, before Brody—would dote on her, them, their relationship, say things like 'you're so lucky' and 'how do you do it' and 'if I could only find a man like him.' Melissa doesn't disagree, but these friends don't see the little things that pile up to bug her sometimes—the trash unemptied, the doors unlocked, the toilet unflushed, the tiny tasks that stack up like bricks to build a life that Trevor can't be bothered to do. It's not that he's malicious or selfish. Okay, maybe a little selfish, Melissa thinks, the grin returning. She has long admitted to herself that some of it is petty frustration, the fact that she leaves the house with him at the kitchen table, his desk, the couch and returns from work to find him parked in the same place, no evidence of work or even movement.

She carries the bags through the living room, notes Brody's blocks strewn over the floor, and continues on to the kitchen, putting the groceries on the counter.

"Trevor?" she calls. "Brody?"

They must be in the yard, she thinks, and when she thinks of the yard, a pulse pushes through her so violently that she nearly doubles over. Her bruises ache and throb, at least one popping to spill yellow goo and trails of sand on her skin.

When she's at work, gone from the house, the thoughts of the yard—the hole—disappear, and her sores calm to bruises that ache dully, and she can almost push it aside. Almost forget that a hole in the backyard drove the previous homeowner bonkers enough to try to bury himself in the sand.

One of the bags tipped when she lurched, and on her way out the door, she steps on an errant orange, the squish and tear of the rind under her foot causing her stomach to lurch. For her to feel a pulse, a pain like that, something must be happening. Trevor and Brody must be by the hole, with the hole—fuck, godforbid—*in* the hole. She pushes through the screen door—*whap crack*—over the side porch and into the grass.

The yard is empty. A meager trail of beer cans, if two can be classified a trail, dots the backyard. Melissa has a vision, a flash of mental clarity, and she is sure that Brody is down in the pit floating in a limitless dark sandy nothing, torn and shredded like Walter Henderson's legs. She rushes to the back of the yard, calling for them both.

"Trevor?! Brody?! Oh fuck. Please be okay, please be okay, please."

She's panting when she gets to the pit, falls to her knees, and tears at the sand like a wild animal. For a moment, she entertains the idea of inserting her whole head—putting her face into the sand to scream, to yell, to call out for her lost family—then thinks better of it, remembers again the image of Walter Henderson, the shredded slacks, the screams.

Alone. If she can't get them out, she's alone in this house, on this street, in a neighborhood she's not sure she wanted to move to in the first place. Alone to pay the mortgage, mow the lawn, live, grow old and die, all with a sucking, breathing, living *thing* a hundred feet away in the backyard.

A sucking, breathing, living thing that ate her family.

A branch, a twig, something snaps behind her, and with her attention turned that way, she's conscious of the symphony of noises she had previously missed. Rustling leaves, crunching branches, heavy breathing, low crying.

She stands and turns from the hole, the sucking, breathing, living thing, and there on the bank is her husband. His hair is matted to his forehead with sweat, his mouth open and panting. On his right hand is the remnant of a flannel shirt, the fabric soaked dark with what she assumes must be blood. In his hands is a bundle, a mess of twigs and leaves and dirt covered in a wash of red.

Their only son. Her son. Brody.

Brody alive. Brody reborn. Brody dirt-caked, scratched, and covered in blood.

21.

AROUND THEM, the sounds of the hospital form an anxious hymn, a chorus of beeps and whirrs and rings and voices that meld into a single droned note in Trevor's mind. They sit on a bench in the hallway outside Brody's room, each with a cup of coffee between their feet, the greasy sheen on top of the dark liquid eerily visible in the fluorescent hospital lights.

Trevor's hand is a mummy, the face of the invisible man, a sterile cocoon, the bee-sting pain thankfully dulled by painkillers. He rolls a new bottle in his good hand—this one with his own name on it—and lives in the irony of receiving a new bottle of painkillers for losing the old one.

"What is happening, Trevor?" Melissa finally asks. She was the voice of calm, the pragmatic, organizational force that got them in the car, spoke calmly to both of them, got them to the hospital, filled out paperwork.

Now she looks to Trevor like she hasn't slept in days, the bags under her eyes a full set of luggage. She leans forward to pick up the cup of coffee from between her legs, grimaces when she takes a sip.

He hadn't even tried to explain on the way here, and she hadn't asked, and now he finds himself at a loss, any words he could come up with inadequate to describe the horrible afternoon in a way she would understand.

He stares at the white-wrapped bulb of his right hand, wonders how he's going to type with any kind of rhythm now that it's deformed.

87

Certain in his mind, concrete, is the idea that Brody will sing like a canary, possessed by the hole or not, sell him up the river, and tell everyone that Daddy kicked him down the bank on purpose, so for the moment, he maintains his stunned silence.

"The fingers—your hand—it was the hole, wasn't it?"

He lowers his head, picks up his coffee, and this is answer enough.

When the doctor had asked if he had the digits, he'd slowly shook his head, said that he fainted when the clippers he'd lopped them off with by accident cut through his bone, came to hearing his son wail at the bottom of the bank, and the adrenaline had buoyed him through the next few minutes until Melissa found them bloodied at the top of the edge of the yard.

Melissa lowers her voice, leans in close. "What do you think will crawl back out in exchange?"

He looks up, but can't find surprise in his mind or his heart. So she knows, then, he thinks. If Nick knows about the hole, then there must be other neighbors who know something, some distorted version of what's back there. Melissa had implied the other night on Nick's stoop that she knew what happened to Walt, so the Fran woman must have told her something, told her everything, who knows. Or maybe she's jumping to conclusions about the origins of the knife. Or maybe—and this thought chills him more than he can express—the hole has created a cloak of thoughts, a shared knowledge base that both of them, having given to it, can tap into, access. Maybe it's not that she found out about the pit's haunting trading post style exchange system but that she simply *knows*, has known, doesn't know how she found out.

He sips the coffee, the bitter liquid matching his heart.

"I'm not sure. Maybe nothing since I didn't give them willingly."

"I'm not sure that matters," she says, sitting back on the hard bench, clutching the paper cup between her knees like a lifeline, a tether to the sane and rational world.

"It feels like a haunting," she says after a while, the words hanging around them like the ghost he thinks she's suggesting. "Like something's trapped down there and is mad about it, doesn't want us in the house, doesn't want us on the land, whatever. I can feel a change in myself when I'm not there—I'm clearer, sharper—but when I'm in the house, I'm foggy, open to suggestion, feel like I'm not fully in control of myself." She turns to him, finally, talks to his peripheral vision. "Does any of that make sense?"

He smiles, not because any of this is funny but because this, this conversation, is maybe what they should have been doing all along, could have saved them some grief, kept their boy from the hospital. Communication has never been a downfall of their relationship, but something is flying between them, cutting them off.

"It makes total sense," he says. "Almost like something is getting between us, turning us against each other."

He waits a beat before laying it on the table, going for broke.

"It had Brody."

Her eyes grow wide, and her voice shrinks to a whisper, harsh and secretive.

"What the fuck do you mean it had him?"

He tells her about reaching his hand into the pit, about Brody circling him, smiling, his eyes clouded by something inhuman. He leaves out the pills, the kick, says he tripped near the top and tumbled off the edge.

Sitting back again, she rubs the bridge of her nose, her eyes closed, breathing heavy. "Trevor, I think we need to go. We need to get out of there."

"I can't," he says, and means it, means it with his whole heart, knows somewhere deep inside that it's the truth. Beyond some pig-headed stubborn need to see what comes out next as the result of his fingers, he doesn't think he is physically able.

"We have to," she says, turning fully now, facing him with her whole body, one leg pulled up onto the bench.

"This has been weird so far—fucking batshit—but now, *now,* it's violent. It's not just a wild thing that we can't explain. Things have been . . . happening." She trails off, a vacant look in her eye, and Trevor wonders what thing she's going to reveal, bruises, dreams, suggestive voices. He sees her hand go to her leg like an anxious tick and smiles.

"Bruises?"

Slowly, cautiously, her head nods, but she makes no move to pull up a shirt, unbuckle her pants to show him.

He casts a furtive look around the hallway, finds no one paying attention to them, and lifts his shirt. A hand flies to her mouth and she gasps, so he lowers it quickly to conceal his pulsing torso. Grains of sand float down out of his shirt onto the bench, he wipes them to the floor with the back of his hand.

"When I said I can't leave, I really think I can't," he says, and she's crying now, her hand still over her mouth, the tears running down her hand. "But maybe, if yours are still bruises, you should go. Take Brody and leave for a while, just until I sort this out, figure out some sort of solution."

Her head shakes, and she opens her mouth to protest, but he silences her with a finger. She grabs it and moves it from her face, gentle but firm, and squeezes it in her lap. Tears leak from the corners of her eyes and she sighs, a long, heavy sigh like putting your backpack down at the top of the mountain.

"Goddamn it, Trevor, I want to leave, but I wanted you to at least fight me on it." She looks down at her lap, at his good hand cradled there. "I want us to either stay as a family or go as a family. It doesn't feel right splitting up."

"Nick, the neighbor from down the block, he's the one who found Walter when he . . . you know." He waves his hand to indicate the unspoken. She nods to say she understands, has been told, or maybe just *knows.* "I'll get together with him and try to think of something, try to figure something out to cover it, get rid of it, *kill* it, I guess."

"God, Trevor, what the fuck did we do? We never should have moved here."

"I'll take care of it. It'll be okay, I promise," he says, pulling her into a hug. Her tears dampen his shirt. He rubs her head gently with his bandaged hand.

They stay like that for a long moment, and that's how the doctor finds them, gets their attention with a soft clearing of his throat.

"Mr. and Mrs. Davis?"

Both nod, break apart. The doctor smiles.

"Brody is going to be just fine, it's mostly scratches and bruises. We checked him out for a concussion, for anything broken, but all seems to be in working order. For the pain, just use baby aspirin or low-strength Tylenol." He sees the orange bottle in Trevor's hand. "No need for two pain pill prescriptions. I'll get the paperwork sorted and to the front desk, and you two can take him home. I'm sure it's been a long day for him."

The doctor turns to leave, and Trevor sighs in relief, the tension of a possible accusation leaving his muscles.

"Oh, I also wanted to say," the doctor says, turning back to them, emotional whiplash seizing Trevor's chest.

"He said he was playing in the back of the yard and fell and that 'Daddy saved him.' You're his new hero, Mr. Davis."

Trevor's mouth falls open, his heart swells.

"All the same, I'd put in that fence sooner than later."

22.

MELISSA AND BRODY leave in the morning.

"We're going on an adventure. We're going to stay in a motel," she says, clipping him into his car seat.

"Is Daddy coming?" he asks, but she shuts the door without answering, leaves him gesturing and wriggling in the seat behind the window.

"I wish you were coming with us," she says, pulls at the collar of Trevor's unbuttoned flannel shirt, pulls him in for a kiss.

"I'll be along as soon as I figure this out," he says, and from the corner of his eye, he can see a truck pull onto Hollenbach—a trailer with a prefab shed pulled behind.

She follows his gaze, allows a smile to slip through the cracks.

"I think this is a good start. I just hope to hell it works." She kisses him again, long and hard, then dips into the car. He watches her comfort Brody, check his buckles, then put the car in drive and pull away from the house. He waves at the back of her head then turns to wave the truck into the drive, directing it with the good hand not swaddled in gauze.

Both sides of the truck open, and two workers tumble out—matching men with salt-and-pepper stubble in matching work pants and blue polo shirts.

"Mr. Davis, yeah?" The non-driver approaches him with a clipboard of paperwork, a pen taped to the metal hinge. "Gonna need your signature at the spots with an x."

The driver starts undoing buckles on the trailer, loosening the straps that hold the shed in place. The first guy takes the clipboard back and checks the signatures, a toothpick dancing between his lips. When he's assured that the paperwork is in order, he tosses the clipboard onto the seat of the truck and turns back to Trevor.

"So where's this going, then?"

Trevor leads Toothpick around the side of the house, through the yard, and to the back. They stop by the edge of the sand, and Trevor points with his bandaged hand.

"I was thinking it could go right around here."

Toothpick looks up at Trevor, back down at the patch of sand in the yard.

"They told us at dispatch that you'd already poured the pad. You know this would hold up much better on a concrete pad, yeah?"

Trevor nods, acknowledging his lie to the store rep, the dispatch.

"Yeah, I know, but pouring a pad is so expensive, and it's a prefab with a floor, so I figure I could get it in, get it situated, and do the pad when I have the money for it."

Toothpick looks to the other shed, the original shed, a perfectly serviceable structure at the back of the property that sits on its own concrete pad. He seems to acknowledge the situation and decide he doesn't care. He shakes his head, looks back at Trevor.

"Is that leveling sand at least? That'll help the thing not sit on a tilt, keep it normal, ya know," he gestures with one hand, plucks the toothpick with the other. "'Til you get a chance to pour a pad."

"Oh definitely, yeah, that's leveling sand," Trevor lies, and Toothpick either buys it or doesn't care, so he turns to wave the driver in and they back up the trailer into the yard.

They lower the shed into place and Trevor feels a great anxiety pulse through him, a feeling that he thinks, feels, *knows* is the mind of the pit, and he allows himself a small smile.

"Yo, buddy, c'mon! Get your dog out of the way!" Toothpick hollers over the noise of the trailer, the idling engine of the truck, and Trevor looks up to see a mangy canine nipping at their heels, going between the workers like a wolf trying to fell a large animal by severing its tendon.

Trevor runs to the animal, his guard up but his hand outstretched, calling to it to get out from under the lowering shed.

"Hey, fella, c'mon. Come here!"

The dog shuffles out from underfoot, and Trevor gets a good look at it, the patchy fur, the mangled mouth with teeth exposed. Chunks of skin show through the thinning coat, and Trevor can see bugs, worms, maggots, something vile crawling over the skin of the animal beneath the hair. He reaches out tentatively and grabs the collar, chancing that the ancient leather won't break beneath his hand, and catches a glance at the dangling tag.

Louis.

Trevor doesn't have to imagine where the dog came from, doesn't have to second-guess that it crawled, struggled, out of the hole—maybe overnight, maybe this morning—emerging fully formed from his lawn like a morbid stillbirth, a whining animal forced from the birth canal of sand at the back of the yard. He suppresses a shudder.

"C'mon, Louis. Let's get you cleaned up."

Trevor leaves the men to their work and shuffles the dog into the house.

23.

TREVOR STANDS IN the living room, in the house, his house, alone, the silence draped over him like a shroud. Louis—bathed, scrubbed, cleaned—is tied to the large pine in the yard, his snout resting over his crossed paws as he naps in the grass, one eye creeping open to survey anything passing by.

Trevor brought him inside and cleaned him up, doing his best to ignore the wounds around the legs, the missing patches of skin, the bugs that crawled over the fur of his face to enter and exit his mouth via the exposed gums and teeth. Though he'd nipped at the heels of Toothpick and the driver, his attitude changed inside the house, and he gave in to the bath with pleasure, seeming to relish the warm water and soap, Trevor's hands scrubbing and petting.

The pills and knife had belonged to Walt Henderson— the label and Nick had confirmed as much—offerings to the hole. Trevor shudders at the idea of Walt surrendering his dog—his presumed best friend—to the void, feels pity for the man whose house he now occupies, a man who thought he had no choice but to give everything he had to the thing living on his property.

Not like I can't relate, Trevor thinks, and opens the fridge in search of a beer, something to take the edge off, something to keep him from thinking of his family, now gone, holed up in a motel. To keep him from thinking of the dog, some half-living mutt tied to the tree out back. To keep him from thinking of his missing fingers—a blood trade for that very dog—his gaping sores, his cursed house, his haunted yard.

He pushes past leftovers in tupperware containers, pureed carrots in jars, old condiments, and packaged cheese.

No beer.

He slams the fridge door, thinks of running out for beer, eyes the new painkillers resting on the kitchen counter. The weight is good in his hand, a comforting presence that replaces the feeling of Walt's pills. Under his shirt, his sores weep for the covering of the hole, the new shed, the abomination placed upon the god of the yard. Sand trickles from his torso to pile on the floor, the grains gritty underfoot. He opens the bottle and removes a pill, swallows it dry, exits the kitchen into the yard.

That afternoon, he had moved some tools from the old shed to the new one. There was no practical reason for this, the new shed was a symbol, a marker of his emancipation from the pull, the pulse, the call of the hole, and he didn't have enough tools to spread between two sheds anyway.

Still something tugged at him, some urge had caused him to move a few things to the new shed, a
shovel

axe

hedge trimmer
and he gazes now upon his yard, his conquered yard, his kingdom that he now owns anew.

Standing, observing, he searches his mind for the pull, the throb, the thrum of the hole, and comes up empty. Maybe this is the solution, he thinks, then reminds himself of what Nick told him, of the concrete, the cinder blocks, the limitless materials that Nick and Walt sent into the hole with no measurable change.

A vision appears to him, a waking dream of the shed collapsing, imploding into itself to be sucked into the yard, a splintered mess of fabricated wood, shingles, siding.

GIVE UNTO US

Trevor looks to the shed, the yard, the dog, then turns to walk through his newly conquered yard to the bar next door.

24.

NEON, LIKE THE neon of the signs outside the bar, soaks the interior as well.

It's a dive, Trevor thinks, but smiles, regrets it taking him this long to stop in, to make an appearance at a watering hole so close to his home. Back at the apartment, before Brody, he would stop in at Tom's, the bar down the street, whenever he had a slow day working from home or Melissa worked late, practically living there in the evenings during tax season.

Then came Brody.

But now he's gone, isn't he? Brody and Melissa both, at least for a while, and as far as he can tell, the shed has solved the problem of the hole, has at least put up a roadblock to him wasting his time sending things into it, feeding it, sitting by it in a drunken haze until the sun comes up. He could turn around, go home—take a six pack with him, a compromise—and pull that unfinished manuscript from his desk drawer, tinker with it. He could pull his guitar from the office closet where he unceremoniously shoved it during the move, strum around on it, learn some new songs, maybe even start writing one. He could do it. Go home and do a hobby, art for art's sake, the way he was before, the way he was before he got old enough for everything to need an end goal. A book, an album, a trip, a day not wasted on something as trivial as relaxing. All before time started piling up on him, sand in the hourglass, sand pouring on his head until he drowns under the weight of it. Back before a hole grew inside him, a hole he tries desperately to fill with music, work, typing, beer, exercise, when he should be filling that hole with family, with *living*.

He takes an empty stool at the bar.

The barroom bears more than a passing similarity, at least in tone, to Nick's house. If Nick added some glowing beer signs, he thinks, they could be siblings, not twins, not quite, but from the same brood certainly. He wonders if one developer built the whole block, got the idea for the stretch of houses along the river and commandeered the entire thing. Such a wild risk building so many structures on ground that could eventually surrender to the silt, the bank, and slide right into the water. Soft earth, not the best for building, even the shed guys—Driver and Toothpick— had been concerned about that, a small shed, an inconsequential structure that would hold no occupants, just a couple tools—

shovel

axe

hedge trimmers

—and was really only there to block the hole anyway. The hole. He can't feel it, can he? The pull, the ache, the rampant desire to send things careening into an endless, bottomless void. This thought pulls him from his internal rambling and he pats his torso, his shoulder.

Dry.

No weeping, oozing, bleeding.

He smiles and looks up to find a man staring at him, his head cocked gently to the side like examining him, waiting to see what he'll do next.

"What can I get ya, fella?"

"Beer," he says, too excitedly. The bartender doesn't step back but looks like he wants to. "No, whiskey. Ah, fuck it, we're celebrating. Make it a Maker's and a Pabst. Please."

He's grinning like a fool and can tell that it makes the

bartender uneasy, but the man is a consummate professional.

"You got it, pal." He pulls a frosty mug from a freezer, fills it on an angle, lets the head fall out and hit the trough underneath. It slides across the bar to land in front of Trevor, a coaster following. When he pulls a bottle of Maker's Mark from the shelf, Trevor indicates that he should pour for himself also, so he pulls two shot glasses up from beneath the worn wood bar and fills them.

"What are we celebrating tonight, then, fella?" the bartender asks, holding up his shot glass.

"Trevor," Trevor says, holding his in kind.

The bartender nods. "Bob."

"Well, Bob, let's just say I got some good health news, and that I'm in remission."

"I'll drink to that," Bob says, and they do, the glasses knocking a flam on the bartop. He pours another.

"Hey, I'd love to get in on that," someone says, and a stool scrapes beside Trevor. Turning, he sees a young-looking man, mid-thirties or so, pulling himself onto the stool, both hands on the bar to steady him. "What we drinking?"

Bob holds up the bottle of Maker's, and the man nods.

Bob fills a third glass, and they cheers them.

"To your health, then," the stranger says, and Trevor is feeling the effect of the shots, a warm sensation crawling down his throat and into his belly, his newly emancipated belly living in his free body in the bar next to his house with the yard, his not-quite-die-in-it sized yard, but his yard, his newly reclaimed, conquered yard.

"I'm Trevor," he says, and in the haze of the whiskey he reaches out to shake with his bandaged hand.

"Whoa, what happened there, buddy?"

"Oh," he says, not yet drunk enough to not be embarrassed, "I lost two of my fingers in, uh, an accident."

The stranger's face flushes, and his eyes lock on the bandages.

"How bad is it? Can I see it?"

"Vern, that isn't really appropriate," Bob says, but he looks around at the otherwise empty barroom, and Vern seems to see him do it, and they both shrug and look back to Trevor.

"You can see it," he says, taking a long drag of his beer, "but the next shot is on you."

Vern smacks his hand on the bar, and everyone jumps at the sound. He lets out a hoot. "I'll take you up on that."

Bob sets up the shots, including himself, and Trevor begins to unwrap the mummy casing on his hand. The whiskey is doing its job of dulling the pain, but he notices a throb as he undoes the wrapping and makes a mental note to grab another pill when he gets back to the house.

"What the . . . " Vern says, and Trevor knows he's talking about the sand starting to trickle out of the folds of gauze. He wonders if the whole wrapping is full to bursting with sand, if maybe his whole hand is sand now, consumed and gone—is his penance for trying to cover the hole, to forget about it, defeat it—but he keeps pulling the wrapping, and it's only a thin stream of grains that comes out until he finally gets to the flesh and looks upon his maimed hand for the first time.

Under the bandages, he expects to see swelling, the yellow, green, black bruising he's familiar with, expects to see the stitches the hospital used to seal the sockets of his missing digits. The hand is swollen, almost twice its normal size, but the discoloration is a pattern and color that he's sure is only significant to him, the coloring matching the bruises on his torso, shoulder, arms.

At the terminus of his missing fingers, where he expects a sewn-together patch of flesh, are two holes, sores, pulsing and weeping. Coming out of them is not the pus that he expects, but the sand that trickles and grinds underfoot, grains pushing out of the sockets with each dry, grisly pulse.

"Holy shit, man! What the hell is going on here?" Vern

101

leans in close with no hesitation, raises a hand like he means to touch Trevor's hand, his eyes starting to glaze over. Trevor pulls back the hand, covers it with the gauze, and his stomach lurches with a familiar knotting, his chest slicks with the hungry, expecting pus of his sores.

"I cut them off with a pair of hedge trimmers. I must have gotten it dirty when I was doing yard work earlier," Trevor says, and can tell the lie falls deaf on the two men. Bob is equally enraptured, saying nothing, just staring ahead at the empty barroom, and Trevor wonders what of this he'll remember, if this is something he'll tell future patrons about, but a fog rolls into Trevor's brain and takes control of his thoughts and convinces him it doesn't matter. All that fills his mind is thoughts of the lie, of the *hedge trimmers*

shovel

axe

back in the shed, the shed, the shed with the thin wooden floor sitting on top of the hole, the breathing, sucking, living god in his yard that he must get back to, must fall to in supplication, must feed.

"What kind of hedge trimmers does something like that in one go?" Vern asks, his eyes still glassy, his voice dripping with awe.

"I live right next door. They're in the shed. I can show you," Trevor says.

Vern nods, slack-jawed, and they down the whiskey and stand from their stools.

From behind the bar, Bob waves with a dishtowel, not turning, his foggy eyes still fixed on the empty barroom.

25.

MELISSA SITS ON the curb outside a fleabag motel on the outskirts of town, the flickering light of the vacancy sign bouncing off the cellophane of the pack of Marlboros she stopped and bought on the way here.

She hasn't smoked since she and Trevor got married, it being an unspoken agreement that they would quit together by the wedding, but figures she's justified now. Inside the room, the door cracked so she can hear any disturbance, Brody sleeps, the long few days catching up to him and knocking him down for the count. She's thankful for this, this respite after the short drive full of talking, of nonsense questions, of garbled nonsense emotions filtered through the not yet formed two-year-old brain, mouth, tongue.

For all the excitement, none of it seems to be sticking to him, and for that she's grateful. Not like his verbal abilities are such that he could articulate the slow-burn trauma he's likely harboring from almost being thrown, then being kicked—

Wait, how does she know that?

Brody told the doctor he fell, and Trevor—did he tell her he kicked Brody? She doesn't think so, but the memory is there, burned into her brain like remembering a scene from a tv show. She's there with them: Brody circling Trevor, her husband's foot kangarooing out to launch their son off the edge of the world.

Just as it had come, the vision dissipates, and she's back, back with herself, back on the parking curb in front of the half-opened hotel room.

The lighter flares in front of her face, dots swimming in her vision when it surrenders back to the relative dark. She takes a long drag, holds it, and devolves into a coughing fit. Covering her mouth so as not to wake Brody, she stands and walks into the parking lot, paces in the flickering light of the motel sign.

She and Trevor met smoking on the sidewalk in the quad outside Jerry DeStefano's Halloween party sophomore year. They'd both come alone, both had roommates that urged them out of their respective dorms, coaxed them into being social. So that was their version of social: Zorro and Courtney Love smoking together outside the Corman building, ignoring the party that was raging mere feet from them.

She didn't know then, couldn't know, that this rough-around-the-edges boy was a snowball turning to avalanche, a quick slide picking up disparate pieces of culture as he careened through the world. Structured, pragmatic, and reserved, she fell for his impulsive traits almost instantly. She couldn't see that these impulses, this obsessive need to do something, say something, *be* something was a cancer, a hole growing inside him that he could never fill—could never hope to fill—but would try with art, booze, sex, music, writing.

He was drunk that night, they both were, but he still managed to get her cigarette lit, the lighter a swaying flame like the back row of a Guns N' Roses gig, threatening to catch her hair, soaked with too much hairspray, threatening to send them both to hell in a blaze of glory right there on the quad.

Outside the motel, pacing in the dark, she laughs, takes a more confident drag.

Back at the door to the room, she stomps out the butt on the sidewalk, listens for sounds of Brody stirring. She slips back inside, shuts the door against the chill and the glow of the office, the vacancy sign. As the door's closing, she catches a glimpse of Brody sleeping in the last sliver of light, and shakes her head, spiders crawling inside it, creeping through her brain and filling her thoughts with dread.

"No, no, no," she chants, a mantra, a chorus, a hymn to quell the dark. Her hand finds a light switch and she doesn't care if he wakes up, watches him blink in the new light, coming forward from the fog of sleep. She rolls him slightly, rolls him to see the arm that she caught sight of in the dying light of the parking lot, and there her fear is confirmed.

On Brody's bicep, dark purple and rimmed with green, pulses a bruise.

This isn't supposed to be happening, she took them away, pulled them from the house, the pit, Trevor is taking care of it, all of this is supposed to be getting better, and how did he get this, anyway? And what are these?

"Mommy?"

He's awake now, but she doesn't care, is flipping him over, is pulling his shirt roughly over his head, is looking for more bruises, is looking for evidence that this is a Bruise, a capital B possessed Bruise, is looking for matching ones, is trying to match the arm one with the bruises he collected tumbling down the hill. That's it, that's what this is, just a bruise from his fall. He fell forty feet for Chrissakes. He was kicked. Trevor kicked him, connected with his chest and sent him flying because, because, because *what?*

Because he was already possessed by the hole.

Possessed.

Melissa hates that word, has hated that word this whole time, hasn't wanted to admit to herself that that's what this is, that's what all of this is, a possession, a haunting, that they're possessed, their house is haunted.

If this is a ghost, it's nothing like anything she's

familiar with, nothing that the books or tv or movies prepared her for, and isn't that deeply, intrinsically, cosmically unfair?

Under his shirt, Brody is bruised, but these are the hill bruises, the kick bruises, the fall bruises, and she knows, doesn't want to but *knows* the arm one is different. She places a hand on it, gently holds Brody's arm, and under the skin she feels the pulse, the pulse that should be in Brody's wrist, neck, thumb but is living here in the top of his arm, the warmth pushing through the skin to live in her hand.

"Brody, when did you get this?" she asks, and when she looks up to Brody he's not crying, he's not saying his names for her, he's not doing anything but staring, a smile starting to creep into the corners of his young mouth.

"Brody are you okay—" she starts to say, but a pain wracks her leg with such intensity that she lurches backward, falls into a chair and pushes it aside on her way to the ground. From her sitting position, even in the dingy light of the motel overheads, she can see the thigh of her jeans darkening, the 'spot growing as the wound beneath it seeps. The pain crawls from her leg to her belly and takes up residence, fills her with a warmth and ache that nearly doubles her over.

Something must be happening, she thinks, something at the house is happening. Trevor is failing. Trevor is in the hole. Trevor is halfway down the rabbit hole of sand flailing, screaming, crying, dying.

She pushes up from her sitting position using the toppled chair as a brace and, level with the bed now, she can see that Brody has swung his legs off the bed and is sitting, just sitting, staring at her with vacancy, *vacancy like the motel has,* in his eyes. On his arm, the bruise is nearly two inches raised now and she watches it pulse, throb, and burst. The pus she's now so familiar with dripping, crawling, oozing down her son's tiny arm to soak the already-stained comforter.

After the pus comes a push from the bruise, and sand trickles from the hole in Brody's arm, the sand in the hourglass counting down the time they have left.

With no options left, nothing in her mind but saving Brody, saving Trevor, saving her family, she scoops Brody, still smiling, into her arms and bursts through the motel door.

Behind them, marking their trail from the motel room to the car, is a trail of pus, blood, and sand, like a great wounded snail has materialized, spent the night, and driven away.

26

TREVOR LEADS VERN across the gravel lot and into their yard, the neon at their backs casting long distorted shadows. The moment they step into the grass, he can feel a pull, like the momentum of a self-propelled mower, the influence seeping over him like a gossamer shroud, enveloping him, warming him.

"I always wondered who lived in this place. I've been coming to this bar for a long time. You lived here long?"

"Nah, just a few weeks," Trevor says, and in that moment, move-in day seems years ago, another life. And in a way, he supposes it is.

Something moves in the shadows and both men jump. The movement is followed by a ragged bark.

"Ah, shit, sorry to scare you, Vern. I forgot I left Louis tied up out here."

Louis creeps out from the shadows of the pines, and in the moonlight, his haunting features nearly glow. The skin under the bare fur patches is ghostly white, the teeth showing through the sides of his ragged mouth, a grisly yellow.

"Jesus, man, what happened to him?"

"He caught a bad case of the mange."

Trevor is getting good at lying, at spinning a web of fabrication, or maybe it's the influence of the pit, still pulsing beneath the shed, using its invisible tendrils to manipulate his mind into bringing it its next meal.

Meal?

Trevor wonders when he realized that the hole needs to eat, that the giving back of items is a token appreciation, and guesses he's always known, that it's a film of knowledge seeping over him and Melissa and Brody.

Melissa.

Brody.

For the first time since they left, he misses them, wants them here with him. *If I feed it,* he thinks, *they can come back, all of this will be calm again.*

"Trevor?"

Trevor turns back to Vern, blinking.

"What?"

"The dog, man. I was saying that I've never seen a case of the mange like that. Have you had him down to the vet?"

Trevor wants to be done with this, this stall, this roadblock, between him and everything coming back together, everything coming back to normal again.

"Yeah, I drug him down. I've got some pills, a cream that I rub into the gnarly spots, but he's just got to tough it out, unfortunately."

Vern shakes his head, the thought almost too much for him.

"Well, shit. I'm sorry, man. I hope that things start to get better for him, especially once it starts to get truly cold out here at night."

They're at the shed, Trevor's whiskey fingers fumbling with the keys, the Master Lock.

"I'm going to get him situated in this shed soon. That's why I put it here," he lies. "Wanted it closer to the house so he didn't feel quite so disconnected."

Vern, without knowing it, mimics Toothpick from earlier that afternoon, looks from one shed to the other, notes their distance, shakes his head like it doesn't matter.

A click signals that the right key has found home in the lock, and Trevor pulls down on the hasp and pockets it. There's no electricity in the shed, but Trevor clicks on a lantern—did he bring that out here? He doesn't remember bringing it here, but maybe it's always been here—and the small wooden structure fills with soft light.

Leaned against the bare, pressed-wood wall are the only tools he brought in here, his
shovel

hedge trimmers

axe

and he watches Vern look around, watches him notice the emptiness, watches the uneasiness creep into his eyes the same way Louis emerged from the shadows.

A nervous chuckle escapes Vern's lips. "Didn't get a chance to move much in here, huh?" He chuckles again, more volume this time, like he's trying to convince himself that this is normal, this is all normal, nothing to see here.

When Vern looks up, the hedge trimmers are in Trevor's hands somehow, and he wonders how he missed it, wonders if the tool jumped from the floor to land in his neighbor's hands.

Trevor leans against the door, hopes his blocking of it is as subtle to Vern as he thinks.

"Is that the trimmer?" Vern says, and now his voice drips with caution, with unease, with nerves.

Trevor holds the tool out, so Vern can examine it in the soft light of the lantern. He snicks it open, the sound ominous and loud in the enclosed space.

"This is it," Trevor says. He sticks one of the remaining fingers of his maimed hand into the blades, the gauze bandage dropped to the floor of the shed, the stumps of his index and middle finger dripping sand, oozing pus. They start to weep when they enter the shed, the proximity to the hole bringing them back to grisly life.

"See, I got too close to the blades while I was trimming the pine tree," Trevor says, traces the blade with the skin of his ring finger.

Vern stares at the stumps, mesmerized, his eyes glazing at the yellow of the pus seeping from Trevor's hand.

"That makes sense," he says, his words dripping like

molasses from his slack mouth. "You must have just got them in the way." He raises his hand, and Trevor removes his, leaves the blades of the trimmer open for Vern. "I imagine you must have just . . . gotten too . . . too close . . . " The tip of Vern's finger grazes the blade, and Trevor leans forward, kicks the blade back to the crotch of Vern's hand, and squeezes the blades shut.

Pain—sudden and white hot—pulls Vern from his hypnosis, and he wails. Trevor pushes him back against the wall of the shed, dropping the trimmers to press his mangled right hand—instinct taking the lead over practicality—to Vern's mouth. His breath is hot and steaming against Trevor's hands, Vern's eyes wide and pus and sand clumping in strange viscous dribbles against his chin.

Vern's hands grope blindly—find the knife at Trevor's waist. Trevor slaps his hand away, and Vern goes for it again, this time with more vigor, and this time the knife is in Trevor's hand, flashes in the lantern light before disappearing into Vern's belly. Instead of a scream, Vern grunts in surprise, like having the air punched out of him, like falling from the monkey bars at school and being unable to breathe. His body tries to lurch backward, to escape the knife, but the wall catches him. He opens his mouth to scream, and Trevor presses his mangled hand harder to his mouth to catch it, keep it.

Even in his addled, desperate state, Trevor recognizes that a line has been crossed, that he saw the line in the sand and jumped across with both feet, that this is an act you don't come back from.

Full speed ahead, no breaks, damn the man.

His finger, his shoulder, his torso pulse and ooze.

His hand still on the knife, he twists, watches the fight go out of Vern, feels the weight of his body pull him to the floor of the shed. On the ground he breathes, ragged, hitching breaths that threaten to fill the small space with hot air.

JUSTIN LUTZ

If Trevor's fingers brought the dog, pulled it up, living—or at least undead, he thinks—from the bosom of the earth, what will other body parts bring? Trevor nearly drools at the prospect, the idea filling him with warmth even as Vern grows cold on the thin floor of the fabricated shed.

When he's sure that Vern is gone, when the jaw goes slack, the eyes roll back, and the fingers on his throbbing, mangled right hand can find no pulse, Trevor pulls the axe from its resting place against the wall and sets in chopping apart the floor, splintering it with sweeping arcs as wide as his grin.

27.

IN THE CAR, Brody says nothing for the entirety of the drive. His body is slicked with the seemingly endless pus pouring from his arm, is smeared with blood and sand from Melissa's hasty retreat.

Have to get to the house, have to save Trevor, have to reunite the family.

Maybe they just don't understand the hole yet, maybe they're not giving

feeding

it the right things, maybe there's a way that they can coexist, cohabitate, live together. If this thing is as old as Melissa thinks, assumes, *knows,* then someone must have learned to live with it, someone must have figured it out, so why not them?

If the choice is safety alone—*and is that a choice?*—or compromising as a family, how far would she need to drive, how many states would she need to drag Brody across before the sores close, before the light returns to his vacant eyes? Melissa chooses family. Chooses their unit. Chooses their holy union. Their fighting chance.

Her shoe slips on the gas pedal, the pus from her leg seeping down her jeans to slick the floor of the car. It would be just perfect, just her luck, to resign to coming back, joining the pit, surrendering to the hole, only for an effect of that same hole to send them careening off the road, flipping in midair until the car comes to rest on the roof, their bodies smashed, safety glass sticking to their fluid-soaked bodies.

113

Pulsing, living, breathing in her mind is another thought: what if the pit needs one of them?

Would she send Trevor, send herself, into the pit to save Brody? To clear his skin and fill his eyes—Trevor's eyes—and bring his life hurtling back, to give him his own fighting chance? She thinks she would, thinks she will.

A vision fills her mind. A vision of her swinging a shovel at Trevor's head, the swing stunted in the tiny shed; her knocking him out cold; her chopping, digging, through the floor of the shed to get to the hole; her fingernails peeling back clean off her fingers as she pulls at the particle board with her hands, fresh blood joining the old, dried pus already caked around her cuticles; feeding him to the hole, inch by inch, his head going first, so he doesn't get a chance to scream, to protest, to convince her otherwise.

This can't be a premonition, can't be real, has to be a projection of the pit, the hole, the living, breathing, sucking thing. She hasn't been inside the shed—has only seen it arrive on the back of the truck, didn't even see it placed in the yard, didn't see Trevor move anything into it—so she can't be imagining the inside of it, can't be imagining the floor, the walls, Trevor.

Trevor.

Have to keep clear, have to keep focused, have to save Trevor.

She looks at the bag on the passenger seat, the bag she bought on her way to the motel almost as if she knew she would come back, knew all along she would be back to make her stand, their stand.

Their fighting chance.

She pulls the item from the bag and tucks it into her jeans pocket next to the cigarettes, the lighter.

Gravel crunches under the tires, and she pulls into the drive too fast, too fast, the brakes causing her to skid an extra inch or two on the loose stones. She slams the car into park and wrenches the keys from the ignition, hops out and circles back to Brody's door. Is he safer in the car? She could lock the car, come back for him when this is done to pluck him from his seat and take him to safety. On the other hand, she's seen his interest in the buckles of the car seat, his nascent understanding of how they work. If something happens to her and he can't get out on his own, how long will the air in the car stay fresh? Will he have enough to breathe before someone finds him and lets him out? She's heard the stories, heeded the warnings about leaving your child in the car, but has no actual working knowledge of the interior environment of parked vehicles.

"Fuck it," she says and pulls his door open. Her hands work fast, and he's unbuckled, out of the seat, in her arms, across the front lawn, and in the house. "Trevor?" She knows he's not in here but calls out of instinct, a habit, a stereotyped honey-I'm-home.

Passing through the house, it's almost as if she's pulled by a wire, an invisible cord connecting her to the yard, the shed, the hole, whatever hell awaits her, whatever hell was signaled by the cramps in her belly, the sores on her legs.

She wants to wipe Brody clean, scrub the blood and pus from his tiny body, his still baby skin, but another cramp, another wave of pulsing throbs from her sores tells her there's no time, no time, this is all happening right now—might have already happened—is just so much sand in the hourglass.

Brody's jumper is in the living room, the living room she never got around to putting plants in, the un-living room, and she plops him in and secures him with the straps, buckles she's sure he can free himself from if the mood strikes. He shows no such mood, which is almost worse, just bounces gently, his tiny, socked feet against the hardwood, those dead, vacant eyes staring up at her void of any feeling or acknowledgement.

"I'll be right back," she says to him, but she doesn't believe it, doesn't believe anything, doesn't know if the real Brody in there can hear her at all.

One more look, one glance, at the thing that might be

her son bouncing an ominous rhythm in his jumper, then she's through the kitchen, out the screen door—*whap crack*—and into the yard.

Tied to one of the pines, standing just outside the ring of shadow cast by the bar lights, is a dog. She doesn't think she has the mental bandwidth to handle that right now, but she thinks, feels, *knows* it's a product of the hole, of the living, breathing, sucking thing, and whether it's an agent of the pit or not, she can't be bothered to care. It's tied up, thank god for small blessings, and it doesn't bark or snarl or growl, just stands in the patch of dull light, its teeth showing through the mangled skin of its jaw.

Turning from the dog, she sees the shed, the monolith that now commands the center of the yard. Trevor couldn't have gotten lights hooked up in there, not in a day, and there are no extension cords running from the house, but a dull light peeks through the lines of the door all the same. Also, if she focuses, she thinks she can hear chopping sounds but not wood, not any material she's familiar with.

Her feet are like lead, the grass molasses, and she crosses the yard in a daze. She doesn't know how long it takes her to reach the shed

sand in the hourglass

but her hand is resting on the handle now, the aluminum cool in her grasp.

Slowly, slowly, she turns the handle and opens the door.

28.

A LANTERN, that's the source of the light, and it's the only sane part of the tableau the door opens upon, so it's what her mind fixes to first. There are no shelves, but a lantern hangs from a hook in the ceiling, casting soft light down on the rest of the shed.

Casts soft light down on Trevor.

Gone are his shirt and pants, his underwear soaked with blood and pus. His skin is slicked with it, but she thinks it's mostly blood, smeared about him like hasty warpaint, like sigils, like tribute.

The floor is hacked away, just like her vision, and she gags, the taste of the Burger King she and Brody stopped for chasing the smoky aftertaste of the cigarette from the parking lot, and she wretches when she sees what Trevor is doing.

In his hand is an arm, the bone showing through what used to be the elbow. The bone is splintered and broken, the result of an amateur amputation. She watches him hover the arm over the hole in the floor, the hole that exposes the pit, blood dripping from the severed appendage into the sand below. The pit itself is growing, pulsing, writhing, the sand

the sand worked its way back up

now expanded to cover the floor of the shed, piled around Trevor's bare feet, piled around the body in the corner.

Oh god. The body in the corner. A man she doesn't

117

recognize—or the remains of him, a torso with a lolling head, the head still with a trucker cap perched atop it. Gone are both arms, both legs, all lopped off with similar lack of skill, the bones shining eerie white through the cloak of blood and viscera that lives at the end of each stump.

Matching the white of the bone is the handle of the knife, the offering from the pit, sticking out of the center of the man like a planted flag, his torso the claimed territory.

Unable to hold it, to stay silent anymore, she gasps, and that is when Trevor notices her.

Until now, his face is turned from her, the back of his head all that she sees, and when he turns, he drops the arm into the pit, and she swears she sees the sand reach up like to meet it, to receive it.

And his face, his face, oh god, his *face*.

"Melissa, come here. I figured it out. It's all okay," is what she thinks he says, what she thinks he means to say, what she hears in her head, but it comes out all backwards, twisted, garbled and distorted because of the state of his face.

Pus streams from his nose in great gushes, a little kid on the sledding hill with snot turned on like a faucet. His eyes are still there, still Trevor's eyes—*Brody's eyes*—but the sockets they lie in are puffy and swollen. His mouth is a sore, a weeping, pulsing sore that throbs like tasting the air, like the sore on his shoulder first did, like her wounds do, like the wound on Brody. Sand dribbles from the corners of his mouth and, though his mouth is open, gaping, she can't see to his throat, so thick is the mix of pus and blood and sand.

She tries to run, wants to run, needs to run, but her sore-covered legs betray her, carry her fully into the shed, cause her to close the door behind her. Underfoot, she can feel the sand moving, swirling, rising.

"Oh god, Trevor. What have you done," she says, and it's less of a question than a musing, and even saying it, her heart isn't in it, her will destroyed. He reaches out with his mangled hand, and she can see that this too is leaking sand—the sockets where his fingers once were weeping grains of it

sand in the hourglass

that join the mass on the floor.

Even in her revulsion, the part of her that belongs to the pit, the possessed part, the haunted part, carries her forward, carries her to meet him in the center of the tiny structure under the swinging lantern.

Trevor leans forward—he was always taller, was always leaning down to kiss her—and his mouth meets hers, consumes hers, locks to her face in a sucking, throbbing connection.

Consumed, she has time to think, *that's the word for it, this thing has consumed him, consumed us, our family, all of it,* and then her mouth begins to fill with wet, glopping sand. It falls down her throat, packs in around her teeth, and she flails against him, slaps his leprous torso, her hands slick with the juices of him.

Below them, the sand begins to swirl in a sort of dance, a pattern that sweeps the body in the corner off the floor and into the center, into the pit.

It gave us a shovel first, Melissa thinks, *a toy shovel, a joke, it knew we couldn't dig ourselves out.*

Her slicked hands paw at the fabric of her jeans—searching, flailing—looking for the quarter stick she bought at the fireworks store next to the motel. The store with the tattooed clerk, his shaved head glistening under the fluorescents. The illegal firework she bought from his trunk when she asked what he had with the most power.

"Oh, you'll blow the shit out of near anything with this, yeah," he had said, handing her the paper sack with the quarter sticks in it.

It works up under her fingers, like

the sand worked its way back up

and slips free of the pocket to land in her hand, brings the lighter with it. She flicks the wheel, prays for it to catch.

JUSTIN LUTZ

Trevor takes a step toward the hole, the living, breathing, sucking thing, Melissa stepping with him. She presses the hissing cylinder into his hand, and they hold it there, grasp it together, carry this with them together. For them, for this, for all of this, for Brody.

The sand on the floor rises even as they begin to sink, their limbs falling into the warm moisture of the pit.

It throbs, like a question, and Trevor answers, gives it everything.

29.

ONCE. The block shudders once. A soft reverberation that echoes under the river, causes small ripples to form on the surface of the water. Above ground, the only sound is a soft *whump*, an anomaly that stirs a few sleeping bodies but wakes none.

30.

NICK HARPER TAKES his coffee on the porch most days, an old superstition that helps him greet the day outside, breathing the air, engaging. He slept for shit, rolling around in his cocoon of old blankets, the windows open to chill the air in his bedroom.

Silt collects at the bottom of his cup, the one drawback of his old, ragged french press, and when he gets a mouth full of grounds on the last swallow, he leans off the side of the porch to spit in the flower bed like he does every morning.

In his peripheral, just barely, he catches movement— something in the road—and he turns to find a dog and a small child walking down the centerline.

More fucked up than what it is on the surface—a toddler out at first light walking a dog without a leash—is that Nick recognizes this dog.

"Louis?" he says.

It can't be. Walt said Louis ran away, slipped his collar and took off into the wooded canal across Hollenbach, even though Nick always suspected something more sinister.

As Louis rushes toward him, his suspicions are confirmed. The dog, familiar with Nick in life, has a strong memory in death it would seem, and rockets up like to lick his face.

Turning his head away, Nick can smell decay on Louis's breath, the sickly, sweet smell of rot.

"Alright, alright, fella. Good to see you too," he says, cautious to not upset the dog, unsure what it will do next.

Nick pushes Louis down and looks past him to take in the boy.

It's Trevor and Melissa's boy, though Nick can't remember his name, was drunk when he met him, ruffled his hair—far too drunk. The child stands, still, in the center of the road, his eyes not looking up at Nick and Louis but down at the chipping asphalt. Nick bounds from the porch to meet him in the road.

"Hey there, son. What are you doing out here all alone?"

Only when he gets to the boy does he see the full state of him. His clothing is soaked, dyed brown from blood, too much blood, but Nick can tell almost intuitively that it is not the boy's blood. Smeared in with the blood is a pale green color, creeping mold on bread left too long. Nick grabs the boy's arm and the boy winces, and under his fingers, Nick can feel the lumps of bruises and a grit like sandpaper.

"C'mon, buddy, let's get you inside. Let's get you cleaned up."

31.

THERE'S NO ANSWER on the number Trevor gave him, and Nick is not surprised. The moment he found the dog and the boy in the road, he knew that the panic was over, whatever was happening or had happened could not be stopped, and he heard no screaming in the wind, so he took his time.

The boy—*Brody*, he had whispered—sleeps on the cowboy couch in the living room, the patchy version of Louis curled on the floor like a sentry. It's early for liquor, but the bottle is uncorked all the same, the buffalo glass in his hand. He doesn't want to go over there, doesn't want to discover what there is to discover, but knows he has to, knows that he will understand better than most.

He thinks of Walt, thinks of the screams, and drains his glass.

Nick shudders then leaves the house, walks west up the center of the road.

Silence hangs over the Davis house, a silence he can hear internally as if the world that vibrates like a plucked guitar string has been muted.

Nick doesn't bother with the house, knows better than that, and is surprised to see the shed. He almost chuckles.

"Damn, Trevor, not a bad idea," he says to himself, but the mirth is short lived. He crosses the yard to the shed, puts his hand on the cold aluminum handle.

Finding Walt changed him, changed the way he

thought about the world, and something inside tells him that this will be much the same.

Nick turns the handle and the door is shoved from his grasp, torn free by the floor-to-ceiling sand, cool to the touch, that cascades out of the shed like a wave.

ACKNOWLEDGEMENTS

In the spring of 2017, mowing the yard in our new house, I found a pile of sand that seemed to be growing out of the ground. After pointing it out to Lois, we thought it might be a septic mound, then a night of rain revealed a child's shovel and we decided, much like Trevor initially does, that the previous owners must have dumped a sandbox there, never bothered with cleanup, but I began to think about what else might crawl out of the sand, and if anything else might crawl back into it.

Thanks, first and foremost, are due to Max Booth III and Lori Michelle: for publishing this book, for pulling it up off the floor, dusting it off, and giving it life.

This writing thing is only as good as the people you surround yourself with, so eternal thanks to the Void Collective: Sam Richard, Evan Dean Shelton, Edwin Talmadge Callihan, Michael Tichy, Matthew Mitchell, and OF Cieri.

John Boden, Ambrose Tardive, and Amy Mastrangelo read drafts of this book and offered advice and notes that made it better.

Jeremiah Stoyer told me which fireworks might most effectively blow apart a sand mound and whether one could buy them legally in Pennsylvania.

Thanks to Matthew Revert for the beautiful cover, and thanks to Cris Crude for my author illustration.

Last and not least, thanks always and forever to my wife Lois: for encouraging me at every turn, for helping carve out time for me to write, for not being weirded out when this house on the river closely resembled our house on the river, for everything. I would pitch every bit of myself, piece by piece, into a carnivorous sand pit if it meant we could live there together.

ABOUT THE AUTHOR

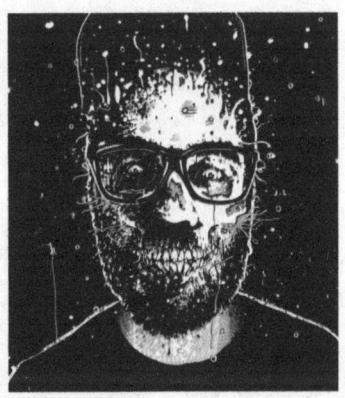

Justin Lutz is a Splatterpunk Award nominated writer, musician, and screen printer living on the river in Pennsylvania with his wife and cats. He is the author of the novella *Gemini Rising*, the charity novelette *ACAB Includes Animal Control*, and the short story collection *Gone To Seed*. His short work has appeared in *Teenage Grave, Gravely Unusual,* and *Ghoulish Tales*. As a member of the Void Collective he helps conjure Voidcon and is one of six to collectively summon the Void Haus. He believes in Bigfoot, strong coffee, and the healing power of Bruce Springsteen.

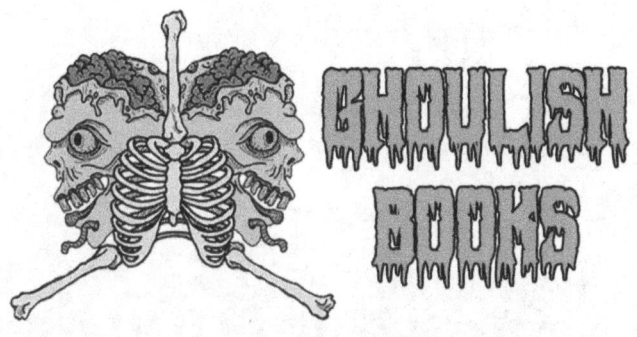

Patreon:
www.patreon.com/ghoulishbooks

Website:
www.Ghoulish.rip

Facebook:
www.facebook.com/GhoulishBooks

Twitter:
@GhoulishBooks

Instagram:
@GhoulishBookstore

Linktree:
linktr.ee/ghoulishbooks